PANIC IN PAXTON PARK

A PAXTON PARK MYSTERY BOOK 2

J. A. WHITING

To hear about new books and book sales, please sign up for my mailing list at:

www.jawhitingbooks.com

❀ Created with Vellum

For my family with love

1

Shelly, Juliet, and Jay, short for Jayne, sat around the little table on Shelly's front porch eating slices of apple and cinnamon cake and drinking iced tea and lemonade. Shelly's Calico cat, Justice, sat on the porch railing listening to the human's chatter and watching the people stroll by on the sidewalk. It had been nearly a month since two murders in the mountain resort town of Paxton Park had been solved and Shelly's breaks and bruises from the killer's attack on her were healing well.

"I'm feeling almost back to normal. The doctor said I can start biking for exercise now." With a sparkle in her blue eyes, Shelly gave her friends a little grin. "I didn't tell him I started biking to work a week ago."

"Well, you're careful when you bike and it's only a mile to the bakery," Juliet said.

Ever the pragmatic one, Jay said, "You really should have let Juliet drive you to work until you got the okay. If you fell, you would have delayed the healing process." Forty-three-year-old Jay Landers-Smyth was Juliet's older sister and a twenty-year veteran of the Paxton Park police force. Tall, stocky, and strong, and with a keen intelligence and ability to handle difficult situations, she had gained the affection and respect of the community.

Lifting the last bite of cake from her plate, Juliet said, "This apple cake is one of the best I've ever had." She flashed a smile at Shelly. "Nothing like having a talented baker living in the house right next door to me."

Twenty-eight-year-old Shelly eyed Juliet with mock suspicion. "Sometimes I wonder if my baking skills are the only reason you became friends with me." A recent transplant to Paxton Park, Shelly had been in a horrific automobile accident seven months before accepting a job as a baker at the resort. The accident claimed the life of Shelly's twin sister, Lauren, and Lauren's boyfriend and it left Shelly with physical injuries that still plagued her with occasional pain in one leg and a limp, but it was the hole in her heart from losing Lauren that was the heaviest burden to bear.

The chat turned to the arrest of the perpetrator of the recently solved murder investigation. Juliet, twenty-eight, slender and athletic, had the opposite build of her older sister. She asked Jay, "Did I tell you that Shelly had dreams that gave her clues about the mystery?"

Jay almost dropped her glass. Once she set her drink down on the table and wiped up the spill, she turned to Shelly with a serious gaze. "Did you?"

Shelly gave Juliet a stern look. "No, I didn't."

"That's a big fib," Juliet scolded. "You had dreams and some of the details in them gave hints about what was going on with the case." Addressing the next comment to Jay, she said, "Her twin sister appears to her in the dreams."

Jay straightened and stared at the brunette across from her.

Before Shelly could speak, Jay said, "I've heard about this sort of thing. It happens sometimes after a trauma. People have dreams that provide them with information, or send them a premonition, or point the person to things they're overlooking from daily life. I've read that sometimes in dreams a relative or friend appears to the person as a guide."

"Mine are simple dreams," Shelly protested as she shifted uncomfortably on her seat. "On occasion, my sister shows up in them because I miss her. There isn't any hocus-pocus involved."

"Do you believe in the paranormal?" Jay asked.

Justice stood up, balanced on the porch rail, arched her back, and let out a loud meow.

"I don't know what you mean." Shelly leaned back in her chair subconsciously increasing the distance between herself and the two women.

Juliet said, "You know, like extrasensory perception, being able to see spirits, telekinesis, faith healing, psychic ability."

"Then, no, I don't believe in the paranormal." Shelly crossed her arms over her chest. "Those things are the stuff of campfire stories and horror movies."

Jay spoke gently. "Did you know that police departments sometimes employ psychics to assist with difficult cases?"

Shelly's face lost a bit of its color. "I've heard that, but I thought it was only silliness or rumor or people making it up."

"It's a fact. At times, the assistance of a psychic has been very helpful." Jay could see Shelly's discomfort with the subject. "I have a hard time wrapping my head around such a thing, too, but I know for a fact that now and then police investigations have been helped by people with these unknowable abilities."

"Has your department ever used a psychic?" Juliet's voice was tinged with excitement.

"Not while I've been on the force, so I doubt it," Jay said. "But that doesn't rule out the possibility in the future. There are plenty of things I don't understand or know about and until there's evidence to the contrary on a topic, I believe in keeping an open mind."

Shelly picked up her glass and took a long swallow wishing the conversation would shift to something else. At times, her dreams were unusual and did seem to be trying to send her a message, but she always thought it was her subconscious at work pointing out things she hadn't paid any attention to. It also seemed normal that her sister would appear in her dreams since Lauren had been torn away from Shelly so unexpectedly. Still ... no matter how much she wanted to dismiss the possibility, some dreams did seem to be trying to tell her something.

The one Shelly had last night left her shaken and anxious and she had to get up, make tea, and read for an hour before attempting to fall back to sleep. In the nightmare, Lauren was sitting on the grass near an apple tree sobbing. Shelly was hiking in the woods trying to get to her sister, but so many things blocked her path and impeded her progress ... she navigated a raging river, a thunderstorm broke out with wild wind and pelting rain, and lightening hit the ground not far from Shelly. The rain then turned to snow and, exhausted, she trudged through deep snow drifts.

At last she reached the edge of the field, but a tornado had blown through the area knocking down houses and trees and Shelly had to climb over the rubble trying to find her sister. When she spotted Lauren sitting near the tree, Shelly called out to her.

Lauren raised her head and shook it slowly back and forth and when she lifted her arms out to her sister, Lauren's hands were missing.

Shelly awoke with a start, covered in sweat and trembling.

Sitting on the porch with her friends, thinking about the dream made Shelly's heart race and she gave herself a little shake, rubbed her forehead, and straightened her posture. "So, anything new going on in town? I know there's an annual meeting of some nature conservatory being held at the resort in the next few days."

"I hope they're not a rowdy bunch." Jay shook her head. "People have been known to go a little crazy when they're away at a conference. It will mean more work for the department if a few of the event-goers get out of hand." She added with a smile, "I prefer the peace and quiet and tranquility of the forest and mountains, not the rowdiness of convention goers."

Juliet chuckled. "Then you shouldn't have chosen to live and work in a resort town."

"Maybe I should move somewhere off the grid," Jay joked.

"Then you'd be out of a job," Shelly teased. "There probably aren't many career opportunities in the deep woods, and definitely no jobs in law enforcement."

"I guess I'm stuck here then." Jay smiled as she finished her apple cake.

"If you're free tomorrow around 5pm," Juliet said to Shelly, "and you feel up to it, I'm leading a hiking tour for a group of tourists up to the Crooked Forest." The forest was a good-sized grove of trees on the south side of the mountain where the pines had grown into weird shapes with the trunks coming out of the ground and bending at ninety-degree angles. The trees then grow horizontally for about four to nine feet and then bend and grow upright again.

Juliet said, "We're going to the waterfall area and the granite quarry, along the streams and fields, and then into the forest. It's a big group and I could use your help. It wouldn't be strenuous at all ... we'll be moving slowly as some members of the group aren't in great physical shape."

"I'd be glad to go along." As Shelly nodded, her long, light brown hair moved over her shoulders. "It would be nice to go for a hike after I finish up at work. I haven't been on the trails since I got hurt." Her eyes darkened as she recalled the attack on her life. "It sounds like a good way to start getting back in shape."

Jay swallowed the last of her iced tea. "I'd better get back to the station. I have a mound of paperwork to get done. Let's hope things stay quiet around here like the past two weeks have been so I can make a dent in the work."

Jay's phone buzzed with an incoming call and she stood and walked down the porch steps to take it while Juliet talked to Shelly about taking tomorrow's group kayaking on the lake if time allowed.

A wave of anxiety washed over Shelly when Jay's phone had vibrated with the new call and she was only half-listening to Juliet while trying to make out what Jay was saying. Unease bubbled through her veins and she could barely force herself to stay sitting at the table.

Justice watched Jay holding the phone to her ear and, with her ears flat against the top of her head, the cat let out a long, low hiss.

Clicking off from the call, Jay returned to the porch wearing a worried expression. As she picked up the keys to her squad car from the table, she said, "I need to scoot."

"What's wrong?" Juliet asked picking up on the sudden change in her sister's mood.

"Just some police business."

"You don't look happy about it." Juliet noticed the look of worry on Jay's face and the shift in her bearing.

"I'm not happy about it." Jay's facial muscles tensed and she took in a long breath. "I'm hoping it's a false alarm."

Even though Jay was nearly fifteen years older, Juliet always worried about her big sister's safety. "Is it something serious?"

Jay forced a smile. "Probably not." She looked to Shelly and thanked her for the cake and tea before hurrying away to her police car parked at the curb.

When the vehicle zoomed away and turned onto the main street of town, Juliet turned to her friend with a look of distress. "Something happened. Something bad. I can see it on Jay's face."

Shelly didn't need to see Jay's face to sense trouble descending on the town. Her body had flooded with the same terrible emotions she'd experienced during last night's dream and it made her want to pack her bags and run far away from Paxton Park.

2

Shelly and Juliet strolled the aisles of the market located at the end of Shelly's street picking up a few things for dinner that night. Carrying the Italian bread, a variety of vegetables, a box of spaghetti, and a bottle of sparkling cranberry juice to the checkout, the young women saw a group of people gathered around the cashier and the owner of the store.

"The police are at the house right now. I saw them as I drove by." A delivery man had carried in a large box from his truck and got sucked into the conversation.

Clay, a short, spry, gray-haired man who had lived in town all of his life was gesturing animatedly. "I was at Matt's Garage and he had the police scanner on. That's how I first heard the news. Then I went to the café. Everyone was talking about it in there."

Chet, the owner of the market, stood with his arms crossed over his chest, nodding gravely. "Kids take off sometimes though. She'll probably be back by tonight."

"What's going on?" Juliet placed the items on the checkout belt and looked from person to person.

"Abby Jackson didn't go home last night," June, the cashier, said. "Mrs. Jackson called the police early this morning."

As she took a candy bar from the display rack and placed it with the other things they were buying, Shelly felt the cold finger of dread running along her skin.

"How old is Abby?" Juliet asked.

"She's eighteen," Clay reported.

"When was she seen last?" Shelly hoped the situation was nothing more than a girl and her boyfriend taking off for a few days together.

Chet said, "Abby was out with her boyfriend last night. She dropped him off at his house. He lives about a block from Abby's parent's house. She drove away and hasn't been seen since. Mrs. Jackson is crazy with worry."

June, a pretty, slender, dark-haired young woman, started to ring up the items on the checkout counter. "Abby doesn't do stuff like this. She's a good kid. I've been in school with her for years. We just graduated high school two months ago."

"Are you friends with Abby?" Juliet asked.

"Not best friends or anything like that," June said. "We're friendly with each other though. I like Abby. She's a nice person."

"What about the boyfriend?" Juliet asked. "He's at home?"

Chet told them, "We've heard that Adam went inside as soon as Abby dropped him off last night. His parents talked to him for a while, he ate some leftovers, and went up to his room."

"He was at home this morning?" Shelly asked.

Chet gave a nod. "He got up early. Adam works part-time at the hardware store. His parents were up, they ate breakfast together, and Adam went to work."

Clay said, "Abby's mother called Adam's house. She said she'd gone to bed at 10pm and when she got up this morning, Abby wasn't at home. Abby's bed hadn't been slept in. Adam's parents told Mrs. Jackson that Abby dropped Adam at the house around 11pm and he'd been at home all night. They hadn't seen Abby at all. That's when Mrs. Jackson called the police."

"Has Abby ever done anything like this before?" Juliet questioned.

June looked at her wide-eyed. "I'd be shocked if she did. Abby wasn't like that."

"I don't know," Clay said. "I didn't hear anything about Abby ever taking off before. I'm heading back to the café. I want to hear the latest. Hopefully, this girl turns up safe and sound, otherwise it might go badly for the town. Those two women murdered a little while ago and now this." The older man pushed the door of the market open and strode away down the sidewalk.

Shelly picked up the grocery bag after paying for the food and she and Juliet left the store to walk home.

"This must be the call Jay got when we were sitting on your front porch." Juliet gave her friend a look. "You didn't have any dreams about this, did you?"

"No, I didn't." Shelly groaned when she answered, but something about the missing girl filled her with the same feelings of anxiety she'd experienced while dreaming last night about trying to find her sister. She gave herself a shake and tried to push that awful dream from her mind. There was no connection between the nightmare and this missing girl.

Juliet tried to take the grocery bag from Shelly, but Shelly wanted to keep carrying it saying she was feeling strong now and didn't need to baby herself anymore. "I want to get back to normal as quickly as I can."

"Clay was right about these events possibly having a bad effect on the town," Juliet said. "The economy will suffer if people don't come to the resort. Too many bad things will scare off the tourists ... people will panic. Maybe the townspeople will, too."

"I wouldn't worry. Abby Jackson will turn up. Maybe she and her boyfriend had an argument and she went off in a huff." Shelly shifted the bag in her arms. She wished she believed what she was telling her friend, but deep down, she had a bad feeling about the eighteen-year-old's disappearance.

"Yeah. Maybe." Then Juliet asked, "Do you want to wander over to the café after we drop off the food? I know it's like rubbernecking ... wanting to know what's going on ... I know its nosy and all that. I just really want to know the news. I can't stop thinking about it. Should we do something to help? Should we form a search party? Where's the car Abby was driving? Has it been found? Are there any clues to where she went?"

"Do you know Abby?" Shelly asked.

"A little. Abby took snowboarding lessons from me last winter. It was a group lesson so I didn't get to know her all that well. I liked her though. She was upbeat and friendly. She worked hard. She's really pretty ... slim, athletic, long blond hair, big brown eyes."

"Abby recently graduated from high school? Do you know if she was going to college?"

Juliet said, "I heard she was accepted at a lot of good schools. I thought someone told me she was going to a school in Boston in the fall."

"So she was smart," Shelly observed.

"Yeah. She was a good athlete, too. She ran, played sports, skied, did a little snowboarding." Juliet said, "I wonder what Jay knows. I'd love to text her, but I won't. I know she must be knee-deep in the middle of all this."

Climbing the steps to her front porch, worry continued to pick at Shelly and she looked pointedly at Juliet. "Why don't we put these things away and head over to the café for a coffee."

Juliet gave a quick nod. "Yes, let's."

~

THE OUTSIDE PATIO of the café was crowded with tourists sitting under table umbrellas chatting and enjoying the hot sunny day in the shadow of the mountains rising in the distance. Juliet knew the regulars would be inside the coffee shop sharing news and information about the town goings-on so they opened the door and found a crowd of people gathered in small groups discussing the missing girl. The air-conditioned space was a lovely contrast to the outside heat and humidity.

Juliet looked around for a familiar face and saw a co-worker standing near the back of the room talking with a few other people. Shelly and Juliet ordered drinks at the counter and carried them over to join the small group.

"Hey, Jules," her coworker, Matt Tucker, greeted Juliet and nodded at Shelly. "Your sister must be up to her neck in this one."

"I haven't talked to her," Juliet admitted. "But I'd guess she's pretty busy right now. What's the news?"

A middle-aged, dark-haired woman spoke. "Abby Jackson is still missing. The car hasn't been found. There's been no sign of her since she drove away from her boyfriend's house last night."

An older man wearing a golf shirt and jeans said, "I put my money on the boyfriend. Cops better take a long, hard look at the young man." He glanced at the others with a grave expression. "It's always the boyfriend."

"But, the boyfriend was at home with his parents, wasn't he?" Juliet asked.

"Was he?" the older man asked. "He came home, talked to the parents, and went up to bed. Who's to say he didn't sneak out of the house later? After the guy went up to his room, his parents didn't see him until morning."

Juliet hadn't thought of that scenario.

Shelly asked, "If the boyfriend did sneak out, what did he do? Rendezvous with Abby somewhere? Abby's car is missing so they must have taken it somewhere if they were together. But why would Adam have gone home if he planned on meeting up with Abby later?"

"Maybe the young man wanted his parents to think he was at home," the older man surmised. "That way, he had an alibi."

"Did Abby and Adam have a fight? Were they going to break up?" the middle-aged woman asked. "Was something wrong between them?"

"No one seems to know anything about that," Matt from the resort said.

Juliet's brow furrowed. "I don't understand how Abby's car hasn't been spotted. If she drove away after dropping Adam at home, she could have driven a long way away from town during the night, but the police must have put out a bulletin to other police departments. Why hasn't anyone seen the car?"

"For one thing," Matt said, "Abby was only reported missing a few hours ago. It takes time to find out a few particulars about her disappearance, it takes more time for the Paxton Park police to decide to alert other departments in the area, and even more time for the other police departments to spread the news. Maybe the car will be found soon."

The older man said, "That car could be in a parking garage somewhere. It will take days to notice it. It could be in someone's garage, for that matter. Good luck finding it, if that's the case. It could also be in a ditch somewhere."

Shelly couldn't help but frown at the man's speculation. "Abby could just be driving around. Maybe she's upset about something. Maybe she needs time to think about things on her own."

"That's wishful thinking," the older man said. "But we can hope that's the case."

A tall, thin man with a long, sharp nose and a pinched face stepped into the café and glanced around at the crowd. When he found who he was looking for, he hurried over to the woman and whispered something close to her ear that made her gasp and cover her mouth. Group by group, the news spread around the café causing other people to gasp or to raise their hands to the sides of their heads, with eyes wide and faces pale.

Matt came back to the group at the back of the coffee shop after hearing from some others what had been reported. His face showed a look of horror and when he spoke, his voice was hoarse. "A little while ago, someone walking on the mountain trails found something." He swallowed, took in a deep breath, and paused.

"Well, what was it?" the older man barked his impatience.

"A severed hand," Matt told them. "There's a ring on one of the fingers similar to one Abby wore."

Juliet gasped at the news and covered her eyes for a few moments.

Shelly's head spun and her heart pounded fast and hard against her chest wall. Her dream. Last night. In it, she was desperately searching for her sister, Lauren.

When she finally found her, both of Lauren's hands were missing.

3

After leaving the café, Juliet suggested a walk on the mountain trail that ran next to the resort to be outside and clear their heads of the news that a hand had been found in the woods. As they walked in the shade of the overhanging branches, the scent of pine drifted by and birdsong floated on the air.

"I always feel better when I'm near the forest," Juliet said. "It calms me. It helps me put things in perspective."

Shelly's mind was still racing from the news they heard at the café. "I love the outdoors, too, but at the moment, I can't say I'm feeling any calmer about what's going on. Should we even be walking in the woods?"

"It's okay. We're only a few yards from the resort

hotel. I can hear people moving around the grounds," Juliet said. "I'm trying to think rationally. Abby must have disappeared because of someone she knows. That's usually how it is."

"The poor girl must be dead." Shelly sighed and bent to walk under a branch hanging over the trail.

Juliet bit her bottom lip for a second and then said, "It seems likely. They found Abby's hand. It isn't going to end well."

"So why do you feel calmer?" Shelly asked. "Abby must have been murdered."

"I feel calmer because what happened must have been caused by some relationship trouble. I don't feel like there's a serial killer or some crazy person walking around looking for victims. Abby and someone she knew must have had a fight. The person lost control and ended up harming Abby."

"We don't know who did this." Shelly explained why she still felt panicked. "We don't know for sure that Abby knew her attacker. It could have been a random act. This whole thing won't be over until they find her body and make an arrest. I feel ... I don't know, I feel on edge about our own safety."

Juliet stopped walking and stared at her friend. "You don't feel safe?"

Shelly gave a slight shrug. "I don't."

"Is there more to your feeling?" Juliet stepped closer to Shelly. "What exactly makes you not feel safe?"

Shelly rolled her eyes. "The small incident of a girl going missing and her severed hand being found in the woods. It doesn't exactly inspire confidence in my surroundings."

Juliet started up the trail and then stopped. "Maybe we shouldn't be out here. Just the two of us."

Looking over her shoulder Shelly said, "Let's go back. We can walk around the grounds of the resort. Sit by the lake."

The two young women strolled along the trails and paths that ran through the trees, but were close to the resort buildings and weren't isolated like those in the deeper woods. After an hour's walk, they settled on a bench beside the lake to watch the swimmers and kayakers enjoying the water.

"People don't seem to be impacted by the news," Juliet observed.

Shelly said, "They probably don't know what happened or if they do know, it might not bother them because they're on vacation and have no connection to the missing girl or to the town. They're glossing over it, not paying attention to the trouble. It seems too distant from them. It's nothing that will impact their lives. That's what they think anyway."

"If the person responsible for hurting Abby isn't arrested soon, then it will definitely impact them," Juliet said. "A lot of people won't take part in activities on the mountain. They'll be afraid to be out there on their own. Some will cancel their reservations. Others will leave the resort early. Tourists won't come here if they don't think they're safe."

"Jay and the rest of the police staff must be under a lot of pressure to solve the crime," Shelly said. "The pressure is on top of the normal stress of searching for evidence and clues. I don't think I could do that job."

Juliet sighed. "Neither could I, but Jay seems to have the right personality for police work. I couldn't see her doing anything else."

Shelly started to feel antsy. Although, she wanted to talk to her friend about the dream she had the other night and how it seemed tied to Abby's disappearance, she was uncomfortable bringing it up. It frightened her and Shelly was often afraid to fall asleep, worried she'd have another inexplicable dream. "I wonder how things are going, if the police are making any headway."

Footsteps crunched on the gravel path and when

Shelly glanced up to see who was walking past, she was surprised to see that it was Jay.

"I thought it was you two sitting there. I spotted you from the terrace off the hotel." With a sigh, Jay sat down on the bench.

"You okay?" Juliet asked her sister.

"As good as can be expected. I feel like we've forced a week's worth of work into half a day." Jay rubbed the side of her face.

"Are you making some progress?" Juliet asked and then realized it was a foolish question. Not enough time had passed for any real information to be gathered.

"You must have heard about the unpleasant discovery?" Jay asked. "It seems it's all over town already. Heck, with social media it's probably all over the state by now."

"More likely, the whole country knows about it," Juliet told Jay. "Abby hasn't been found?"

"Not yet." Jay's shoulders seemed to round.

"Who found the ... the hand?" Juliet asked.

"I can't give out a name. It was a townsperson though, taking a walk with a dog. The person had to go to the hospital after talking to us." Jay shook her head. "The person needed something for anxiety, will probably need some therapy, too."

"Did you go out to the area where the limb was found?" Shelly asked.

"I did," Jay said. "The investigators are still out there inspecting the spot and the surroundings. No one is really hopeful about finding much."

"Why were you at the resort hotel?" Juliet asked her sister.

"I had to talk with someone who works there." Jay was always careful not to share important information.

"Who was it?" Juliet pressed.

Jay gave her sister the eye. Juliet loved to pump for details. "It was a human being."

Shelly couldn't help but chuckle over Jay's unspecific response.

"Has Abby's car been sighted or found?" Juliet questioned.

"No, it hasn't. The girl has been missing for almost twenty-four hours. We need to find something soon or the window of opportunity is going to shrink fast." Jay turned a little on the bench, trained her eyes on Shelly, and referred to what Juliet had brought up earlier in the day about the dreams her friend sometimes had. "You haven't had any dreams recently, have you?"

Shelly's face tensed and her eyes grew wide as

she nervously pushed her light brown hair over her shoulder and then shifted her gaze out to the lake.

Jay picked up on the young woman's discomfort, but wasn't sure if Shelly might have had a worrisome dream or if she was just sensitive about the topic.

When Juliet also realized that Shelly was acting uneasy, she leaned forward on the bench to better see her friend. "*Did* you have a dream?"

Shelly was about to dismiss the question when she let out a slight groan and seemed to shrink on the bench next to the two sisters. "I don't know. Maybe." Beads of perspiration showed on Shelly's forehead.

Jay's eyes were like lasers. "You had a dream?" she asked gently.

"Why didn't you tell me?" Juliet's question carried a slightly indignant tone.

"I didn't know how to bring it up," Shelly moaned in her own defense. "I don't understand any of it."

"Can you tell us about it?" Jay asked in an encouraging way.

"It was last night," Shelly began. She went on to describe the dream she'd had about searching for Lauren. "At last I saw her. She was sitting in the dirt, crying." Her throat felt so dry that Shelly had to swallow and cough a few times to clear it. "Lauren saw me trying to reach her and she lifted her arms out to me." Not saying anything for several seconds, Shelly finished her story with one sentence. "Both of Lauren's hands were missing."

The three sat in silence for almost a full minute.

"Did you reach your sister?" Jay asked. "What happened next?"

"I woke up." Shelly blinked and looked over the lush, green lawn leading down to the lake.

"Did you have any idea what had happened to Lauren? How she lost her hands, or why?" Jay's voice was kind.

"No, no idea. She was in distress, alone. She needed my help. She was trying to reach out for me." Shelly passed her hand over her eyes. "I don't know what it means, if anything. It's probably just a coincidence."

"You had this dream last night?" Jay questioned.

"Yes."

Jay kept her face neutral. "Do you know what time it was when you woke up from the dream?"

Shelly was about to shake her head when she remembered something. "When I woke up, Justice was prowling around the bedroom. She jumped up on the side table. It was a little before 2am. Why do you ask about the time?"

"Just wondering," Jay said. "And you've had dreams like this before?"

"A few times. They started shortly after Lauren died, but they strengthened and happened more frequently after moving here from Boston."

Juliet spoke up. "Remember I told you I read that precognition can start after a traumatic event?"

"Precognition? What does that mean?" Shelly asked.

"It's like knowing about an event before it happens," Juliet answered. "It's the ability to see events that will happen in the future."

Leaning forward, Shelly put her elbows on her knees and clutched her head with her hands. "I can't see the future. I only have dreams."

Jay asked, "Would you two come back to the station with me?"

"Why?" A shudder of worry darted through Shelly's body.

"Because ... I need help," Jay said.

4

S helly and Juliet sat in uncomfortable wooden chairs in Jay's cubbyhole of a windowless office in front of the beat-up desk covered with folders, papers, and a laptop.

"I've never been in a police officer's office before." Shelly looked around at the bookcase full of books on police procedure and law.

"It's nothing glamorous, that's for sure," Jay said. "I'm lucky I have a private place to work. Most law enforcement officers have desks side-by-side in one room."

A tall, slim man about thirty years old with dark blond hair poked his head into Jay's office. "Oh, sorry. I didn't realize you had company. Let me know when you're done relaxing."

Jay's face remained neutral, but Shelly and Juliet

saw a flash of annoyance pass over her face. "We're discussing the case, Andrew. What do you need?"

"The chief wants to talk to all of us as a group in five minutes," Andrew told her.

Shelly recognized the man at the same time he noticed her. Detective Andrew Walton had spoken with Shelly about a woman involved in the early-summer murders in Paxton Park and she hadn't cared for him or his rude interview tactics.

"Don't I know you?" the detective said to Shelly.

"We've met," Shelly said cooly.

"You're the baker at the resort, right? Yeah, your sister died in a car accident. I remember."

Shelly winced.

Jay gestured to the door. "If we're all meeting in five minutes, would you mind? Shut it would you, Andrew?"

The detective withdrew and closed the office door.

"I didn't like that guy when I talked with him." Shelly kept her voice down in case the man was lurking in the hall. "He was arrogant and rude and tried to provoke me."

"You hit the nail right on the head with that description of Andrew," Jay said as she tapped on the keyboard of her laptop. "He's best ignored." She looked up, crossed her arms in front of her on the desk, and addressed Shelly. "When I was just out of the police academy, I took a job in Boston for a while where I worked with two detectives on a difficult case. They did great police work and I learned a mountain of stuff from them. They were both professional, smart, dedicated, and honest and I was fortunate to have had their mentorship."

Jay paused for a few moments. "We worked with a psychic. At first, I thought it was ridiculous and didn't understand how these two men could accept such nonsense. When I asked about it, the detectives told me that their job was to solve crimes and they were willing to put their own limitations aside and open themselves to other possibilities. With the help of the psychic, someone was arrested and convicted and sent to prison."

"I didn't know you worked with someone like that," Juliet said with surprise.

"The point is this ... I don't understand paranormal things or skills or whatever, but I am willing to believe in the possibility that there are senses or intuition or abilities that I don't have. I don't need to understand it. If someone has a way to tap into information that isn't available to me, I am more than happy to work with that person to do good for others."

Shelly stared at Jay. "My dreams are just dreams. They're probably just the result of my brain's attempt to cope with the loss of my sister. Things about Lauren and the accident and the loss get mixed up together with things I see and hear in my daily life and end up coming out as strange dreams." Shelly looked down at her hands. "They couldn't possibly mean anything."

"Would you be willing to talk to me about your dreams?" Jay asked.

Shelly met Jay's eyes. "I guess so."

"If I discuss aspects of the case with you, would you be willing to keep that information in confidence?"

Shelly swallowed and gave a nod. "I can do that. But, I think I'll just be wasting your time."

Jay gave the young woman a kind smile. "We'll see."

A knock sounded on the office door. "Meeting time," a voice called.

"I'll be right there," Jay raised her voice a little while keeping her eyes on Shelly. "I wanted to discuss with you some aspects of what we know so far about the missing person's case." She gestured to the door, then stood and gathered some things from her desk. "It will have to wait. I'll be in touch soon."

DECIDING to make dinner another night, Shelly and Juliet sipped drinks in the corner booth at the back of the Irish pub while waiting for their meals to arrive and talked over their meeting with Jay. Shelly was unconvinced that her dreams could be of any help to the investigation and continued to believe that her most recent dream where Lauren's hands were missing was a coincidence and unrelated to the case of the missing girl.

"No one can be sure the hand that was found belongs to Abby Jackson," Shelly said.

Juliet gave her friend the eye. "The hand will have to be matched to DNA from Abby's family to make the final determination, but really? It has to be her hand. The ring on one of the fingers matched the description of Abby's ring. If it's not Abby's hand, then the police have a bigger problem to deal with than only one missing girl."

"True." Shelly took a swallow of her beer.

"And I don't think you can brush off your dream as a matter of coincidence," Juliet said. "You must be picking up on things in the atmosphere ... or something."

Shelly raised an eyebrow.

"You know, sensations or information must float around on the air," Juliet said. "You're able to pick up on it and then it makes itself known through your dreams."

"Do you really believe what you're saying?" Shelly's wore a skeptical look.

"Has anyone in your family ever mentioned any special skills?"

"No. No one."

Juliet smiled. "Until now."

Shelly let out a little groan. "I'm afraid to go to sleep."

Reaching over to touch her friend's hand, Juliet said, "Don't be. The dreams can't hurt you. Think of them as a way to help people. Let them come and when you wake up, you can think about them and decide if there's anything important about them."

"I guess so."

Two women walked over to Shelly and Juliet.

"Hey, you two." Lisa Bennet, the owner of Park Realty, stopped to chat. Her long red, curly hair moved over her shoulders as she turned to her companion, Elizabeth Jones, and made introductions. "Can we join you?" Lisa and Elizabeth slid into the booth.

After a few minutes, the conversation shifted to Abby Jackson.

"Can you believe it?" Lisa asked. "That poor girl."

"My daughter, Caitlin, knows Abby from being on the high school soccer team together," Elizabeth said, her eyes heavy with sadness. "I know Abby's mom. I haven't talked to her yet. I thought it best to wait before giving her a call."

Juliet asked, "Had Caitlin seen Abby recently?"

Elizabeth said, "They've hung out together with a group of friends, gone swimming, kayaking, out for dinner. They're all heading off to college soon, going different ways. It's probably their last summer together." The woman's eyes widened and her bottom lip trembled when she realized how true her statement really was.

"Did your daughter notice anything different about Abby lately?" Juliet asked. "Did she seem upset about anything?"

"Caitlin told me that Abby was having second thoughts about going off to college. She'd considered going into law, but really had no idea what she wanted to study or what career she should aim for.

Abby felt like she didn't want to spend the money without a specific goal in mind."

"Did she want to take some time off before going to college?" Lisa, the Realtor, asked.

"It seems she wanted to work for a year and give her future some thought," Elizabeth said. Realizing that the young girl no longer had a future caused the woman's eyes to tear up. Batting at her cheeks, she apologized for getting emotional and Juliet and Shelly expressed understanding. Elizabeth said, "Abby's mom wasn't on board with her daughter taking time off. She was afraid Abby would end up deciding not to go to school at all."

"Abby was dating Adam Wall?" Juliet asked.

"She was." Elizabeth nodded. "They'd been dating for about three years."

"Did Adam graduate this year? Was he in the same class as your daughter and Abby?"

"Yes, they'd known each other since middle school."

"What about Adam? What are his plans? Is he going to college?" Shelly asked.

"He was accepted at Amherst College," Elizabeth said. "He wants to go on to medical school after he gets his bachelor's degree." The woman rubbed her arm with her hand as if she was warding off a chill.

"They're all such good kids. Smart, hard-working, ambitious. None of them have ever been in trouble. No one would expect anything like this would happen."

"Does your daughter know if Abby and Adam were planning to continue their relationship after leaving for college?" Juliet asked. "Was there any tension between them?"

"Caitlin said they both knew it was a long shot to be able to sustain a long distance relationship. She told me Abby and Adam seemed to be snippy with each other whenever they were out with the group. Abby was going to attend Boston College. Like I said, she'd thought about being a lawyer, but, according to my daughter, she was second-guessing her plans."

"Do you know if Abby had a summer job?" Shelly asked.

"She worked part-time at the gift shop at the resort," Lisa said. "I like the things they carry in there. I buy gifts for my clients from that store so I'm in there quite a bit. I've run into Abby many times this summer at the shop."

"That sounds like a nice summer job," Juliet said. "Out of the heat, not too demanding, helping customers pick out gifts."

Lisa had a funny look on her face.

"Is something wrong?" Shelly asked.

Lisa looked up. "I was just remembering something. I think ... well, I wasn't sure, but..."

"What was it?" Elizabeth asked.

"I was in the store one day early in the summer, I was at the back of the shop in the sale section. I was the only one in there." Lisa's lips were tight. "I thought I saw the owner, Tad Baxter ... he was at the front setting up a display with Abby. I thought I saw him slip his hand up under her skirt."

"You saw him do that?" Elizabeth's voice held an angry tone.

"I thought so, but I'm really not sure. Abby said something to him, I couldn't hear what she said, and then she stormed back to the front counter. On my out, I whispered to her and asked if everything was okay. She told me everything was fine." Lisa narrowed her eyes. "I wonder. Maybe I misinterpreted what I saw?"

Shelly shared a look with Juliet as a wave of anxiety rushed through her veins.

5

I t was late afternoon and almost time for the diner to close when Shelly removed two apple pies from the ovens and placed them on the counter to cool. Baking for the resort diner and the bakery next door to it, required desserts of all kinds as well as breads and muffins and other breakfast items. She'd developed her own granola bar recipes and had recently added them to the menus and they'd proved to be very popular with the hikers, bikers, and boaters.

As Shelly took oats, maple syrup, berries, cinnamon, and different kinds of seeds from the cabinets to begin a new batch of her bestselling bars, Henry, the cook and boss of the diner came into the workroom. In his sixties, Henry, silver-haired, tall, strong, and broad shouldered, ran the place with his wife, Melody.

"That pie sure smells great." Henry wiped his hands on his white apron. "It's taking all my strength to keep away from it."

Shelly chuckled and shook her head. "If you ate everything I bake, your health would be in serious trouble."

"My waistline would be about double the size, too." Henry patted his stomach. "Maybe the resort needs to build a separate baking room just for you so I'm not constantly tempted."

"I don't think that's in their budget this year." Shelly added ingredients to a large glass bowl.

Melody, petite, with short, silver hair, carried some plates into the room, placed them in the dishwasher, and then crossed her arms over her chest and leaned against the counter. "All anyone has been talking about all day is Abby Jackson and her disappearance. How did this happen so soon after those two young women were murdered? Paxton Park has always been quiet, peaceful. Now these terrible things have happened within months." Melody's mouth pulled down at the corners. "It makes me wonder if we should stay here anymore. Is it going to become unsafe?"

Henry clucked soothingly at his wife. "All cities and towns go through periods like this. The world has become more difficult, more unstable, people are stressed, worn thin by bad news and financial issues. We've been lucky here for a long time. Bad things happen everywhere, but the good always outnumbers the bad. We have to remember that."

"Did you know Abby Jackson?" Shelly asked the two long-time residents of the town.

"We know who she is," Melody said. "Or should I say we *knew* who she *was*. Abby seemed like a nice girl. She worked in the gift shop next door." Melody waved her hand to the side of the resort complex. "She did well in school, played sports."

Henry piped up. "We didn't know her well though. Our son is friendly with Abby's father, they play golf, go fishing together from time to time. I can't imagine the pain in that household right now. We tried to think of something to do for the family...." Henry lifted his arms in a helpless gesture.

"The Jacksons were members of the church at the end of Main Street," Melody said. "The congregation is organizing meals to be dropped off to the family. We'll take part in that."

The bell on the café door jingled and a man's voice called," Shelly? Henry?" Jack Graham appeared in the doorway wearing a wide smile and with his blue eyes shining. An outdoorsman in his thirties with chestnut colored hair, Jack, an employee of the resort, had met Shelly about six weeks ago and the two had been enjoying each other's company since.

"You're back early," Shelly said with excitement in her voice as she hurried over to Jack to give him a hug.

"Actually, we're only back for a few hours." Jack wrapped his arm around Shelly's waist. "Bill and I came back for a couple of canoes and some supplies. One of the older canoes sprung a leak this morning and messed up the day's plans."

Jack and two other guides had taken a group of people on a two-week-long, no-electronic devices adventure tour where their base camp was about twenty miles from the town. They'd already been gone for five days. "We got back to camp late yesterday after a long hike on the range and when we gathered this morning for the canoe trip, we discovered one of them was no longer useable."

"How about I make you a nice, juicy hamburger with some home fries on the side?" Henry asked the young man.

"That sounds terrific," Jack told the man.

"Have you heard the news from town?" Melody asked.

"What news?" Jack looked at Shelly.

Shelly let out a sigh and explained what had happened the previous day.

"Her hand was found?" Jack's voice sounded incredulous as he sank down onto one of the stools near the baking counter. "But they haven't found the girl?"

"Not yet," Shelly told him. "The town's in sort of an uproar about it."

"Everyone is talking about it," Melody said. "It's all anyone can focus on."

"Wow. We didn't know about it. It's terrible news." Jack looked from person to person. "Are there any suspects?"

"I bet there are," Shelly said hopefully. "But, it's early in the investigation so no one has heard anything about possible suspects. The police haven't released much information to the press."

"Where was the hand discovered?" Jack asked.

"Near a trail on the south side of the mountain," Henry reported. "Only about a half-mile from here. Someone out walking with a dog found it."

"But how do they know it belongs to Abby? They couldn't have completed DNA testing so soon," Jack said.

"A ring very similar to one Abby wore was on one of the fingers." Henry removed the burger he was cooking for Jack from the grill.

Shelly said, "Nicole told me that the guides have to work in pairs starting today as a safety precaution. At least two guides have to lead the tours now no matter how small the group of tourists."

Jack gratefully accepted the plate of food from Henry. "That makes sense. I'm glad management has instituted the policy and didn't let costs alone determine how they would respond. It sends a good message to all of us working here that our safety is of the highest importance."

"Do any of you know the man who runs the gift shop," Shelly asked. "Someone told me he didn't seem like a very nice guy."

"I never liked him." Melody carried a cup of hot coffee to Jack. "His name is Tad Baxter. He always seemed snooty to me. Always made me feel like I wasn't good enough to shop there."

"I've only been in the store a couple of times," Jack said. "I don't know the man."

Henry looked at Shelly. "Why do you ask about him?"

"Abby worked for him," Shelly said. "Some people have a negative opinion of Mr. Baxter. I wondered if he was trouble."

"A local guy. Interesting." Henry stroked his chin. "Is the perpetrator someone from town or someone here for vacation? I initially thought it might be someone who was visiting the area." Letting out a sigh, he added, "I guess I don't want the person who did this to be someone we know."

The door of the diner opened and then banged shut and Jack's co-worker, Bill, barged into the back-room. "Sorry to interrupt. Jack and I are being called into a meeting with the boss. With what's happened in town yesterday, they're wondering if the adventure tour should be cancelled. They might decide that we have to bring everyone back tonight."

"I don't think it's a good idea." Jack gave his opinion. "This tour has been booked for over six months. It's expensive. Poor reviews will pile in. There are so many of us, I can't believe we'd be in any danger."

"You can tell that to the boss," Bill said. "Everyone I've talked to since we got back has been acting panicky."

"It's only been one day," Shelly said. "It's important to stay level-headed. Let the police do their work. They'll find Abby's body. They'll figure it out and arrest the person responsible."

"But are they going to find her in pieces?" Bill asked. "That's what's making everyone panic. It's some sick killer who thinks it's amusing to murder someone and then chop -"

"Don't say anymore." Melody, her face pale, raised her hand in a halt gesture. "I can't listen to another word."

Shelly walked over to Melody and put her arm around the woman's shoulders. "The police will find the person who did this."

"Not soon enough." Melody's hand shook as she passed it over her eyes.

"Want to help me make the granola bars?" Shelly thought it would help if Melody was able to focus her mind away from crime and murder so they went to the counter to work on forming the bars.

Jack finished his burger and thanked Henry for the food and then gave Shelly a hug goodbye. "I'll let you know if the adventure tour will continue or not. Keep safe."

"You, too." Returning Jack's hug, she gave him a warm smile. "Hurry back."

Jack and Bill left the diner and headed off to their meeting.

"I wish things could go back to the way they were before these crimes made their way into our town," Melody muttered while she rolled the granola ingredients into bar form. "Now, I'm always looking over my shoulder."

When Shelly slipped two cooking sheets into the ovens, she noticed that she'd forgotten to cover and store the two apple pies she'd made. Placing plastic wrap over them, she stared at the crust on top of the pies, golden-colored and lightly sprinkled with sugar. The fragrant scent of cinnamon, nutmeg, and apple floated past her nose.

A vivid image of her sister, Lauren, standing in a field near a toppled tree flashed in Shelly's mind and it sent a wave of panic through her. She shook herself and turned away from the pies, a feeling of weakness surging in her muscles.

Moving quickly to get a glass of water at the sink, Shelly heard her phone buzz in her purse on the kitchen shelf and she stopped to check the call.

It was a text from Juliet.

I just heard that Abby's other hand has been found. It was in the apple orchard on the west side of the mountain, about a mile from town.

Clutching her phone, Shelly glanced over to the apple pies still sitting on the counter and she felt her heart sink way down into her stomach.

6

Justice sat on the steps watching Shelly plant flowers in the border that ran around the front porch. Although Shelly was only renting the cottage, she loved colorful flowers blooming in the front of a home to make it cozy and welcoming and she received permission from the owner to make a garden. Kneeling on the grass, she removed some deep-pink impatiens from their pots and placed them in the holes she'd dug in the ground.

Justice trilled her approval as Shelly drew the soil around the plants with her hand and gently tamped it down.

"You like it, huh, Justice? Me, too." When the young woman sat back on her heels to admire the new garden of pink and white flowers, the cat came down and curled in Shelly's lap, purring. "You sure are a little love bug," Shelly chuckled and ran her hand over the soft, smooth fur.

After a few minutes, her leg began to ache and pulse so she lifted the cat from her lap and pushed herself up to massage the muscles at the back of her thigh. "Enough planting for today," Shelly told the Calico cat. "Let's go fill the watering can and give the flowers a drink."

Justice followed her owner to the back of the house and waited until the watering can was full, then padded softly over the grass behind Shelly to return to the front where the woman tilted the can and watered the base of each new plant. The cat let out a loud meow and Shelly turned to see an older woman in her seventies standing on the sidewalk, holding a grocery bag, looking at the new garden.

"Oh." Shelly startled at seeing the woman just a few feet from her. "I didn't hear you come by."

"The garden looks lovely," the woman smiled. "It makes the cottage look so cheerful."

Shelly thanked the blond-haired woman and watched as the smile disappeared from her face.

"Cheerfulness is in short supply the past few days." Extending her hand to shake, she said, "I'm Nora Blake. I live at the end of the lane in the light blue house with the old-fashioned gingerbread trim."

"I love that house," Shelly beamed. "Your gardens are fantastic. Justice and I take a walk around the neighborhood almost every evening."

"Your cat walks with you? Is she half dog?" the woman kidded.

"She's definitely all cat, but she has some unique aspects to her personality." Shelly looked down at Justice with an admiring smile. "She showed up on my doorstep one day and sort of adopted me."

Nora placed her bag on the sidewalk and leaned down extending her hand so Justice could sniff, then the woman scratched the cat's neck and between her ears. "What a sweet creature." Looking up at Shelly, Nora asked, "Are you working here in town?"

Shelly explained that she'd accepted the job as a baker working at the resort. "I've been renting here for about seven weeks," she said. "Funny, we haven't run into each other before."

"I was away with a friend in Europe for a month. A much needed vacation for both of us. We had a wonderful time." Nora straightened and rubbed her lower back. "I just returned a few days ago. I arrived home and the next day I heard the terrible news about that poor, young girl. What kind of a monster could do such a thing?"

Shelly had no answer for that.

"Her hands?" Nora shook her head in disgust. "Why? Why would someone do that? I suppose that's a ridiculous question. The more important thing to ask is why would someone kill her?"

"Maybe the police will be able to answer that question once they catch the person responsible."

"*If* they catch the person." Nora sighed and then muttered with an angry tone, "That monster had to drag our family into it."

Surprise washed over Shelly's face. "Your family?"

"My family owns Glad Hill Farm on the outskirts of town," Nora said. "It's been in the family forever, for over two hundred years our ancestors have owned that land. My grandparents ran it when I was little, then my parents, now my brother. That killer had to disgrace our property by hiding the poor girl's hand there."

"Your brother was the one who found it?" Shelly asked gently.

"Yes, he was. He's beside himself about it." Nora's face hardened. "He's a nervous wreck, thinking how a murderer has been lurking on our land."

"It must have been awful for him," Shelly told the woman sympathetically.

"Dwayne is a sensitive person, a quiet man. He's been shaken to his core. I'm only glad I returned from my trip in time to be here to support him," Nora said. She looked Shelly in the eye and stepped closer, lowering her voice. "Dwayne had to have a doctor's care. He's been put on tranquilizers and some other meds for the time being. The man couldn't function, that's how upset he was. He has to be able to run the farm."

"He's the supervisor? He has a number of employees?"

"Dwayne and I are joint owners, but he is in charge of the operation. He's the one who knows how to run the place. There are about ten to twenty employees, depending on the time of year. I'm not a farmer. I love the land, but that sort of work is not for me. I was a teacher until I retired."

"You've lived in Paxton Park your whole life?"

"Indeed, I have. I love it here, but I'm often away. My friends have moved to warmer climates. I don't care for the winter anymore."

"What did you teach?"

"I taught high school science for over forty years. I've lived on this street for nearly forty years. My husband and I bought the house shortly after we were married. We raised our son here."

"Does your son still live in town?" Shelly asked.

"Paul lived in New York City, but has recently moved to the farm. There's a small cottage on the property that Dwayne gave him to use as a getaway and a place to stay when he comes to work at the farm. Paul has helped with marketing ideas to bring more people to the farm and orchard ... he's added a corn maze, animals, and a barn that's set up like a general store selling products from the farm, and serving lunch, snacks, drinks, ice cream. It's very popular especially in the autumn."

"It sounds great. I'll have to visit one day. Do you spend much time at the farm?"

"Almost never," Nora said. "I used to handle the bookkeeping for the farm accounts, but it grew too complicated so they hired people with training and experience."

"Does your son have any interest in taking over when your brother retires? Does your brother have children?"

"Dwayne's wife and son died in a car accident many years ago," Nora said.

Shelly winced at the words "car accident."

"My son, Paul, entertains the idea of running the

farm, but it would be strictly as a business manager, he'd hire a farm manager to handle the outdoor work. My son is more like me. He prefers to enjoy the farm without getting his hands dirty in the actual day-to-day running of the place. He's doing more at the farm now, helping Dwayne until my poor brother starts to feel better." Nora shook her head and frowned. "Who knows when that will be. The poor man."

"Did you know Abby Jackson?" Shelly asked.

"She worked part-time at the orchard for several years ... at the corn maze and in the general store. I met her once. She was a pleasant girl, hardworking. Dwayne told me she was wonderful with the customers, especially the children." Nora put her hand up to her throat and a little gasp escaped from her lips. "I just can't believe someone would harm that girl. She can't still be alive. I can't believe someone would kill her."

"Have you talked to people in town?" Shelly asked. "Does anyone have a theory about who might be the killer?"

Nora said, "Plenty of theories, but all idle specu-lation, as far as I can tell. No one knows anything definitive. Abby dropped her boyfriend off at his parent's place and then she headed home ... except she never made it. What happened? Where is her car? Where is her body? Will the police ever figure this out?"

"I hope so," Shelly said. "It may take time, but I think they will. They'll find the answers."

"In the meantime, the town can go into panic mode," Nora said. "I think it's someone from the resort who killed her, someone who was staying there. Abby worked at the resort gift shop this summer. A guest from the resort must have seen her in the gift shop and had the idea to attack her. She was a pretty girl, smart, athletic. Lots of people would find her very attractive. Some nut must have stalked Abby and then when the opportunity presented itself, the person attacked her."

"That could be," Shelly agreed. "The police must be looking into that possibility."

"I hope they are or they're not doing their jobs," Nora huffed. "It's not a very difficult assumption to make." The woman looked to the road when she heard a car engine. "Oh, my brother is here. He's picking me up to go out for dinner."

A small, dark sedan pulled to the curb and a slim, wiry, white-haired man in his seventies got out and approached the women. "I thought you'd be home by now," he said to his sister.

Nora introduced Dwayne and Shelly to one another and they chatted for several minutes ... but without mentioning Abby Jackson or her disappearance. Dwayne welcomed Shelly to the town and asked where she worked.

"I'm a baker at the resort," Shelly told him.

"A baker?" Dwayne asked, "Would you have any interest in doing some contract work? The general store is busy as all get out in the fall and the baker I've employed previously can only work part-time this year. I need someone who can make pies so we have enough to sell in the store. Would you consider it?"

Shelly blinked, surprised by the offer, and unsure of what to say, she stood silently thinking the idea over.

"You don't have to answer right now. Think about it. Maybe come down to the orchard someday, any day at all, and we can talk." Dwayne ran his hand over his forehead. "If I'm not in the barn, ask someone to get me. I haven't been feeling great the past few days. I'm taking some time off."

Nora made eye contact with Shelly. "If you'd consider the job, it would be a huge help to the farm. It would only be for about two or three months, then things slow down. Will you think about it?"

"Sure, I can do that," Shelly said. "No promises, but if I think I can fit it in without the baking impacting my regular job, it might work out."

"If you're able, come by in the next few days," Dwayne suggested. He dabbed at his forehead with a handkerchief. His face seemed to have paled during the few minutes he'd stood talking. "Maybe we can iron something out that will work for both of us. Nice to meet you." He looked at Nora. "Ready to go? I'd like to get home and lie down for a little while."

Nora gave a nod. "Drive past my house so I can drop my off groceries." The older woman shook hands with Shelly. "Nice talking with you." She smiled at Justice who was sitting on the sidewalk next to Shelly's feet. "Goodbye kitty. Maybe I'll see you sometime when you two take your evening walks."

Nora got into Dwayne's car and they drove away down the lane.

"Well, what do you think of that?" Shelly asked the cat.

Justice turned her head and silently watched the vehicle disappear around the corner. She stared after the car swishing her tail slowly back and forth over the ground.

7

D elighted gasps and oohs and aahs filled the air as Juliet and Shelly led the tour group to the beginning of the Crooked Forest. Shelly gave a brief history of the area and the trees and explained the different theories about what might have caused the trunks and limbs to bend in such a way.

"Despite botanists and scientists studying the trees," Juliet said, "we do not have a definitive answer why this particular large grove of pines grew this way."

Someone in the group muttered. "Just like the town police who don't have an answer about the missing girl."

The tour of some of the mountain trails had been postponed for a day while the resort management pondered whether all tours should be called off or if they could proceed. The decision had been made to proceed with caution, however, anyone who had pre-booked a tour would be allowed to cancel without penalty.

The person's comment rubbed Juliet the wrong way and caused a flash of anger to race through her. She knew her sister was working nearly twenty hours a day to solve the mystery of where Abby Jackson was and who had caused her disappearance.

Shelly could see Juliet's facial expression change to one of annoyance so she spoke to the group. "The police in Paxton Park are some of the finest, most dedicated law enforcement officers I've ever met. I know they are working around the clock to solve this crime and are determined to find answers." Gesturing to the path, she added, "Now if we move along this trail, you'll have a wonderful, slightly elevated, picturesque view of all the trees from the other side. Shall we?"

Shelly led the way with Juliet taking up the rear to herd any stragglers back to the group.

"Are you frightened living and working here because of what happened?" An auburn-haired woman in her mid-thirties sidled up next to Shelly.

"No, I'm not." Shelly gave the woman a cheerful

smile. "It's important to be cautious and aware of one's surroundings, but it isn't different from what I've always done. I take precautions, especially when I'm in the woods or out at night."

"That's smart advice." The woman looked over her shoulder to locate her husband, brother, and sister-in-law. "We were golfing yesterday and afterwards we went to the golf course's pub. What a beautiful spot with a huge deck overlooking a lake. We had a drink on the deck and then sat in the screened dining area for lunch. It was terrific." The woman lowered her voice. "When we were out on the deck, I heard some people talking about that poor girl."

Shelly glanced at the woman wondering if she was going to try and pump her for information.

"Anyway, it was four women talking... I'd guess they were in their mid-twenties. They knew the girl and her boyfriend. One of them said her brother was good friends with the boyfriend, Adam something. The woman said her brother told her that Abby had talked to Adam about breaking up. They were each going off to different colleges and Abby thought it was best if they were free to experience college without trying to maintain a long distance relationship. She told Adam that they were too young to make a life-long choice and they should meet and date other people." The auburn-haired woman removed her sunglasses while walking in the shady part of the forest. "Anyway, that woman's brother said Adam was furious about the idea of breaking up. He argued with Abby about it all the time. I heard one of the women say that her brother heard Adam threaten Abby one night."

Shelly looked at the woman with alarm. "What kind of a threat did he make?"

"He told Abby she'd be very sorry if she dumped him."

"But he might have meant that she would regret it when she didn't have Adam as her boyfriend anymore," Shelly said. "It wasn't necessarily a threat of bodily harm. You know it was probably something like, 'you'll miss me when I'm gone', that sort of thing."

"No. That's not the impression I got from the conversation. In fact, what the woman said her brother told her sure sounded like a threat of bodily harm."

"What exactly did the brother tell her?" Shelly's heart pounded hard.

"Adam told Abby that if she broke off with him, she would never be happy without him, that no other man would ever be with her, that she belonged to him."

"That's what you overheard?" Shelly asked.

"It is. I didn't mean to eavesdrop or anything, but that group of women was standing right behind me and I couldn't help but hear what they were saying." The woman pushed a strand of her short hair over her ear. "It gave me the chills. Do you think the brother has talked to the police? What he heard Abby's boyfriend say is important. That boyfriend might have hurt the girl."

"I bet the police talked to Adam's friends." What the woman had told her caused Shelly's mind to race. If the police talked to Adam's friends, would one of them report what Adam had said to Abby about her belonging to him alone? She needed to check with Jay. "Did you catch any of the women's names? Maybe the name of the woman's brother?"

The auburn-haired woman had a pinched, pensive look on her face as she thought back over the conversation she'd overheard. "I'm not sure. Was the friend of Adam named William? I can't be sure, but I think so."

"And what about the women?" Shelly asked. "Did you overhear any of their names?"

"Anna? Maybe that was one of them. I don't really know if that's right."

"I know a police officer from town," Shelly said. "I'll tell the officer what you overheard."

"Oh, that's great. It would make me feel better if they knew. I wondered if I should go to the police myself, but I'm not from around here and they might not appreciate me butting in."

"Can I tell them your name in case they want to talk to you?"

The woman's eyebrows went up. "Me? Oh, no. I don't want to give them my name. I'd prefer to be anonymous. Sorry."

WHEN SHELLY and Juliet finished the trail tour, Shelly shared what the tourist told her about Adam's friend and the veiled threats he supposedly heard Adam say to Abby.

Juliet's eyes were wide. "Oh, wow. Was what Adam said just foolishness that someone might say out of anger or was the threat something he planned to act on if Abby dumped him?"

"I don't know what to think." Shelly opened the passenger side door of Juliet's car. "This woman might have misinterpreted what she heard or she might be making it all up for attention."

"But she wouldn't give you her name." Juliet started the engine. "If she wanted attention wouldn't she go to the police on her own?"

Shelly gave a shrug. "She might not want to make a formal statement. She might have wanted to impress or scare me with her talk about Adam."

"I think we need to tell Jay about this." Juliet backed out of one of the resort parking spots and headed the car down Main Street.

"I agree," Shelly said. "Jay probably knows all this information, but it's better if we tell her, just in case."

"Did Jack return to lead the adventure tour or did their boss cancel it?" Juliet questioned as she slowed for a car trying to turn onto the street.

"He went back," Shelly told her friend. "The boss went back and forth about calling the tour off, but at the last minute he changed his mind and allowed it to go on. Jack wasn't sure it was a good idea."

They rode in silence for a few minutes and then Juliet said, "I know this is a gruesome subject. I can't get it out of my mind though so I need to bring it up. Why would someone remove a person's hands?"

Shelly rested her elbow on the car's middle

console. "Well, I guess one reason would be to make it more difficult to make a positive ID of the body."

"That makes sense. What are other reasons?"

"Maybe it happened in a fit of rage? Or maybe it was something symbolic like making the person seem helpless. Maybe the killer didn't like what the person had done with her hands?"

"What do you mean?" Juliet turned the corner and drove along the lane to where their houses stood side-by-side.

"Maybe Abby hit the killer with her hands or gave the person some rude gesture. If they knew each other, maybe the killer wanted to punish her for something ... maybe he saw her holding hands with another guy. I don't know, I'm guessing. I'm playing pseudo-psychiatrist."

"You're making good points. It makes sense." Juliet nodded as she cut the engine. The two friends remained in the car talking things over. "It kept running through my mind why someone would do something that seems so cruel. Killing Abby was cruel enough."

"The killer might have been hyped-up on drugs or alcohol," Shelly said. "That might have heightened the person's feelings of rage."

Juliet gave Shelly a little smile. "Maybe you

should study to be a cop. Maybe you are in the wrong field."

"No way." Shelly gave a vigorous shake of her head. "I much prefer making tasty food than chasing down monsters. I couldn't handle it."

"On second thought, it's much better for me if you focus on baking. You definitely made the right career choice." Juliet chuckled and raised an eyebrow. "Are you baking anything this evening by any chance?"

"I made a marble cheesecake earlier. Come in and have a piece." Shelly opened the car door to step out.

"You don't need to ask me twice." Juliet locked the car and started after her friend when a black sedan stopped in the street and a man leaned out the window and waved to Shelly.

"I was just at my sister's house. Can you come down to the farm tomorrow? Talk with me about the baking job?" Dwayne called to Shelly from his car.

"Sure. Sounds good," Shelly replied with a wave.

Dwayne nodded and drove away.

"What does he want?" Juliet asked. "Who is he?"

Shelly tried to ignore a feeling of unease as she watched the man heading away down the road. "Come in and I'll tell you all about it."

8

When Shelly arrived at the Glad Hill Farm and Orchard, Dwayne met her in the parking lot and brought her on a tour of the place pointing out the different sections and divisions of the farm. The food barn, brewery, petting zoo, general store, and lake were at one end of the acreage while the orchard stood about a quarter mile from those attractions. Pathways linked the different parts of the farm and visitors strolled together from one end to the other.

"If you'd like to walk along the trails, I can show you the rest of the farm from up on the bluffs," Dwayne said.

After a momentary pause of caution, Shelly decided it would be safe to go with Dwayne to see the rest of the place.

When they reached the top of the hill, Dwayne gestured in different directions. "You can see the part we just left back there. Follow the walkway with your eyes ... that building houses the farm's offices and a little further down the walkway, you can make out my farmhouse. We grow vegetables over in this section and flowers over that way."

Dwayne, dressed in jeans and a long-sleeve shirt and wearing a baseball hat with the name of a tractor company embroidered on the front, said, "You can see the petting zoo is down at the base of the orchard. The kids like that. There are hayrides all year long and in the fall, the corn maze is over there. My sister's son, Paul, is suggesting we expand the brewery since that's a hot thing right now. I don't know, I'm still on the fence about that. I feel like the food barn takes a huge amount of time, what with the preparation of the lunch items, snacks, ice cream, it takes too much work. I prefer working the land than managing a kitchen so I leave that to others." Dwayne moved his hand to the left. "I have a lot of land that's unused. I suggested starting a winery, but Paul wasn't interested. He has his own idea which he decided to jam down my throat. So, that's that."

"I didn't realize your place was so massive."

Shelly shielded her eyes with her hand as she looked out over the acres and acres of property.

"It backs up against the resort land," Dwayne said. "We sold off a bit of our land to them a few years ago. Anyway, that's the farm in a nutshell. Let's go down to the food barn and I'll show you the kitchen baking facilities."

On the way down the hill, Shelly said, "I'm sorry you had an upset here recently. I heard about the sad discovery on your property."

Dwayne's face hardened. "I hope they find the killer and string him up. Imagine killing a girl and ... well, you know what happened. I had the misfortune to be the one who found it. I was out walking the dog. He was really the one who discovered it." Dwayne grunted. "I don't like to speak of it. It's too upsetting."

Shelly murmured some empathetic words to the man. Jay had told her Abby's hand was found just beyond the orchard near the tree line not far from where the farm's vegetables were planted.

"Do you walk with the dog every day?" Shelly asked.

"I try to. It's peaceful, gives me time to think. In the summer, we go early in the morning or at dusk.

It's cooler then." Dwayne noticed Shelly's limp. "Did you hurt your leg?"

"I was in a car accident. This is left over from one of my injuries."

"Will it get better?" Dwayne asked.

"The doctors aren't sure. It doesn't bother me much." Shelly downplayed the effects of the accident. "I can still hike and bike. It gets tired, but I manage."

Dwayne nodded. "Here's the food barn." He led Shelly inside to see an immaculate interior of gleaming wood walls, soaring ceilings, picnic tables, smaller square tables, and fancy chandeliers hanging from the rafters. The space was artfully lit and there were huge windows on one side of the walls. Barn doors on the opposite side were slid back and open to a gorgeous view of the landscape.

"It's beautiful," Shelly said. "I don't know what I expected, but this wasn't it."

"This door leads to the kitchen area." Dwayne opened the door and they stepped into a sparkling commercial kitchen with everything any cook or baker could ever need.

"Wow," was all Shelly could say.

Several people worked in the kitchen and they

welcomed the young woman warmly when Dwayne introduced them to her.

After meeting the other kitchen workers, Dwayne explained the number of pies that would be needed several days out of each week. "You can make your own hours to suit your regular job. There's another baker, but he only works part-time so I need someone else who can do the apple pies." Dwayne pulled out a notebook from a large desk near the wall. "Here's the schedule." He slipped a piece of paper from a folder and handed it to her. "And this shows what your compensation will be."

Shelly had to keep her mouth from dropping open when she saw how much Dwayne planned to pay her.

"We believe in paying well. So if you're interested, you can work right over there. Make two pies. The ingredients and supplies you'll need are in the cabinets or in the fridges." Dwayne gestured. "I'll come back in a while, and try the pies. If they're satisfactory and you feel the pay is fair, then we'll sign a contract. Okay?"

Shelly agreed, Dwayne left to let her bake in peace, and she got down to work preparing the pie crusts and peeling, coring, and cutting up the apples.

Mary, the main chef, walked past Shelly and smiled. "If you need anything, hon, just yell."

Feeling at ease with the people working in the kitchen and comfortable with the baking facility itself, Shelly hoped Dwayne would be pleased with her pies so she could accept the temporary job and save the extra money she'd be making. Deciding on a decorative top crust for the apple pies, she cut strips from the dough to make an intricate lattice top and then used a paring knife to free-hand cut the shapes of Maple and Oak leaves to decorate the edges of the pies. As she was about to place the leaves along the crusts, a man came up beside her. "A work of art."

Shelly looked up to see a tall, slim man in his mid-forties with short dark hair and brown eyes peering over her shoulder.

"I'm Paul Blake. My uncle and mom own the farm. I do marketing for them. The pie looks and smells delicious."

"Nice to meet you." Shelly declined to shake since her hands were doughy and sticky.

"Are you a new baker here?" Paul asked.

Shelly explained the situation and watched Paul's face cloud.

"You've met Dwayne obviously? He explained what he wants to hire you for?"

"He did." Shelly gave a nod.

Paul lowered his voice. "When you get the pies into the oven, would you come outside so we can talk privately?"

A shiver of worry passed over Shelly's skin. "Okay. I won't be long."

Once the pies were in the ovens, she made her way outside to find Paul sitting at a picnic table under a tree tapping away at his phone. Shelly sat opposite the man.

"Thanks for coming out to talk." Dwayne put his phone next to him on the table. "What did you think of Dwayne?"

Shelly's eyebrows went up in surprise at the question. "He's very nice. He gave me a tour of the farm, explained what the job would entail, made me feel at home."

Paul let out a sigh. "Do you know that Dwayne was the one who found the missing girl's hand?"

"I heard that," Shelly told him.

"Dwayne took the discovery hard. It sent him reeling. He's on some medication to help him cope with the upset."

Shelly wasn't sure why the man's medical information needed to be shared with her. "Why are you telling me this?"

"Dwayne's mood can swing wildly throughout the day. Sometimes, he's easy-going and calm, other times, he's on edge, antsy, indecisive, full of anxiety, can't make decisions." Paul leaned his arms on the picnic table. "If you take the job, you'll experience Dwayne's moods. He won't always be nice. He can be mean. It passes, but you'll have to be able to handle it."

"Okay, thanks for letting me know."

"Give it some thought before you sign the contract," Paul warned. "No one knows how long his mood swings will last."

"Is Dwayne going to therapy? Does he see someone who can help him cope?"

Paul snorted. "That will be the day. He won't agree to it. Case closed."

"The medication is helping him?" Shelly asked.

"Somewhat. It varies by the hour." Paul cleared his throat. "I'm concerned about Dwayne being able to handle the demands of the farm especially with the busy fall season approaching. He's been forgetful. He made a costly mistake the other day. It might be time to encourage him to retire."

Shelly said, "But wouldn't retiring make him feel

worse? He wouldn't have the distraction of the work. He seems to really love working the farm."

When she noticed Paul's facial muscles tighten, Shelly worried she might have overstepped by mentioning that the farm work might be helpful to Dwayne.

"We'll see how it goes," Paul said with a dismissive tone and then stood up. "Anyway, it was nice to meet you and best wishes whatever you decide about the baking job." The man headed for the rustic building that housed the office and Shelly returned to the kitchen to check on the pies with the interaction with Paul replaying in her mind.

A few minutes later, Dwayne entered the food barn and made his way to the kitchen. "Just about ready? Smells great in here. Love the smell of baking apple pie." The man spotted the pies on cooling racks and his eyes went wide as he let out an appreciative sound. "Look at those. I've never seen such fine designs. The crust looks amazing."

Picking up a knife, Shelly cut a slice of the dessert, placed it on a small plate, and handed it to Dwayne. "I hope you enjoy it."

Dwayne carried it to a counter and pulled up a stool. With a flourish of his fork, he dug into the crust and the apples and slowly chewed. No expression showed on his face and a flash of disappointment scurried through Shelly.

The man turned to her with a blank expression and then a smile spread wide over his face. "Best apple pie I have ever tasted. If you want it, the job is yours. And I just might try to steal you from the resort. They don't deserve a baker of your talent."

A wave of relief washed over her as her heart swelled from the praise. A little blush even colored her cheeks as Dwayne went on and on about how special she was.

"How about we sign the contract? Unless you'd like to take a day to think it over?" Dwayne asked.

"I don't need to think about it. I'm ready to sign." Shelly shook hands with Dwayne after they each placed their signature on the pages.

Dwayne took one page for his records and Shelly took the other.

"Welcome aboard. The sooner you start the better. Those pies are going to be bestsellers." Heading for the door to leave the kitchen, Dwayne said, "Email the days and times you want to work and I'll make sure you have what you need. Don't bother with the cleanup. We have employees who handle that. Take care, young lady."

Shelly folded her copy of the contract, put it in

her bag, and said goodbye to the kitchen staff who all congratulated her and told her they looked forward to having her around.

Walking out into the sunshine, her stomach experienced a flutter of unease as she recalled Paul's words and she tried to shrug them off.

Dwayne's moods can't be that bad.

Can they?

9

Melody left the diner early in the afternoon due to a headache that would not quit. Before she went home for the day, she asked Shelly to go to the resort gift shop and pick out a present for her sister-in-law's birthday. "I put it off and now I need the gift tomorrow, but I can't drag myself over to the store. Would you mind? I wrote down what I want for her. I'd send Henry, but he'd be at a loss in there and I'm worried he'd get the wrong thing. Would you go? You can leave the gift with Henry and he can bring it home after work."

"See how pretending to be helpless gets me out of doing things?" Henry called from the grill.

"Don't listen to him," Melody said. "He really is helpless."

"I'd be happy to do it. Go home and rest. Maybe take a nap," Shelly suggested.

When Shelly finished the baking for the day, she took her bag and the note from Melody explaining what she wanted from the gift shop and left the diner for the store.

The high-end resort shop was located on the other side of the building complex and the interior was done in shades of cream and light coffee colors. The lighting was soft and inviting and the items for sale were artfully arranged on display tables and shelves. Shelly had never been inside before so she walked slowly around the space admiring the wares.

"Hello," a slim man in his early forties came around the corner from the store room. "Welcome. Is there anything I can help you with?"

Shelly noticed his name tag said "Tad" and realized he was the store manager, the man who had been seen putting his hand under Abby's skirt.

Reaching into her bag and removing the note with the description of the item Melody wanted her to pick up, Shelly handed it to Tad. "My friend would like me to buy this for her. Can you help me find it?"

Tad read the note and led Shelly to a table at the

rear of the shop. "This is what your friend is describing. Touch it. Feel how soft it is."

Shelly moved her hand over the woven throw. "It's beautiful."

Tad checked the note to see which color blanket Melody wanted. "Here's the one she asked for." He handed a soft, light blue and cream-colored blanket to Shelly. "Your friend has excellent taste."

When Shelly saw the price, she nearly gasped. Discretely counting the cash Melody had given her, she was relieved to find there was enough to pay for the handmade throw. "I'll take it."

"Would you like it gift-wrapped?" Tad asked as they headed back to the counter at the front of the shop.

Shelly thought it was a good idea to have the gift wrapped in case Melody still wasn't feeling well. As she watched the man cut some floral wrapping paper to the correct size, she said, "Abby Jackson worked here, didn't she?"

Tad looked up quickly with a surprised look on his face and then smiled to cover his reaction. "Yes, she did. Did you know Abby?"

"I didn't. What was she like? Did you know her well?"

"Well enough, I'd say. She was bright, worked

hard, had a pleasant personality. I enjoyed working with her."

"She was going to college in the fall?"

"Yes, she was."

"Did you know her boyfriend, Adam?" Shelly asked.

"He came in sometimes when Abby was working. I didn't have time to chat with him."

"Did Abby talk about Adam?"

"Sometimes. She'd mention what they'd done together on the weekends or evenings." Tad folded the wrapping paper carefully and reached for a piece of tape.

"Do you think they were happy in their relationship?"

"I really couldn't say."

"Did Abby seem serious about Adam?"

Without looking up, Tad said, "I think she was ready to go off to college and experience more than what a small town like this had to offer."

"Abby talked about that with you?"

"Not really. It was the impression I got from her. I think she was tired of Adam." Tad pulled some ribbon from a roll on the back counter.

"What makes you say so?" Shelly pressed the man for more information.

"Abby didn't seem that excited to see the young man whenever he came in. If he called, she wouldn't answer her phone saying she'd return the call after work."

"Did Abby ever seem upset about anything? Did she mention having an argument with someone?"

Tad raised his head and looked across the room, thinking. "I don't recall anything like that."

"Did you and Abby get along?" Shelly questioned.

"Sure we did, as much as an eighteen-year-old girl and a forty-seven-year-old man could get along. We didn't share a lot in common." Tad finished making the bow and taped it onto the gift box.

"I understand Abby used to work at Glad Hill Farm. I wonder why she changed jobs this summer to work here instead."

Tad smiled. "The farm was hard work. This opportunity was much better for her. An air conditioned space, a more discerning clientele, easier work, and higher pay. What more could she have wanted?"

"I thought she liked working at the farm," Shelly said. "I heard she enjoyed the outdoors. Did Abby tell you how much she made working at Glad Hill?"

"I don't recall." Tad seemed a little annoyed at all the questions.

"I would have thought she'd have stayed at the orchard," Shelly said. "Abby worked there for a few years. Did she ever say anything about someone at the farm being difficult to work with?"

"Not to me she didn't." Tad rang up the sale.

"I'm surprised she left the other job."

"You know she hurt her back?" Tad asked.

Shelly's eyes widened. "I didn't know that. What happened?"

"She was playing sports ... wait, was that it? Or did she fall down? I don't remember." Tad waved his hand around. "In any case, it doesn't matter. The cause isn't what was important. She hurt her spine, she had a cervical injury. It had healed, but it gave her some pain. I think the farm work was too difficult to handle in light of her back injury so she made a change and took the job here this summer."

"That makes sense." Shelly nodded. "Did she complain about her back when she worked?"

Tad said, "No, but I noticed her rubbing at it many times during the day. Sometimes, she sat down while she was changing prices on items or while doing work at the counter. She never complained out loud about it."

"Are you married?" Shelly asked.

"No, I'm not." Tad gave Shelly a look of annoyance and then his expression softened, maybe from thinking the attractive young woman was interested in him. "I'm divorced."

"Did you have any interest in dating Abby?"

"What?" Tad's voice was shrill. "I certainly did not. She was thirty years younger than I am. That would be absurd." The man held Shelly's eyes and a corner of his mouth turned up slightly. "I prefer lovely young *women*, not *girls*."

A feeling of disgust raced through Shelly. She couldn't put her finger on it, but Tad rubbed her the wrong way. His attitude was a little superior and dismissive and his manner bordered on the aggressive side. He held her eyes a little too long, he deliberately brushed hands with her when they exchanged the gift and the cash payment, he got too close and invaded her personal space. It made her uneasy and uncomfortable. She took a step back.

"Are you looking for a job, by any chance?" Tad asked.

"Me? Oh, no." Shelly shook her head. "I'm a baker. I bake for the diner and the resort bakery."

Tad's face lost its smile. "Too bad. You're just the

type of person who would be successful working here."

"How can you tell that?" Shelly's face was hard.

Tad let his eyes rove over Shelly's body and his voice grew deeper when he said, "I can just tell. You sure you don't need a change from baking?"

"I'm very sure. I like my job." Shelly picked up the wrapped gift from the counter and took her change from Tad who again, let his hand linger against hers when she accepted the coins and dollar bill. Pulling her hand back, Shelly took the gift and left the shop in such a hurry that she almost walked right into Juliet outside on the brick walkway.

Apologizing, Shelly let out an exasperated breath and told her friend about the creep of a man who ran the gift shop and what he'd told her about Abby's injured back.

"He sounds like an A-plus creep." Juliet looked over her shoulder to the store. "I'm glad I never go in there. I wonder how Abby hurt herself. We should talk to Jay and let her know what you thought of Terrible Tad. What happened at the farm? Did you get the part-time job?"

A smile spread over Shelly's face. "I did get it and I'm glad about the extra money I'll be making."

"I sense a *but*," Juliet said.

"I talked to Nora's son, Paul, who works at the farm doing marketing for the place. He told me how hard it's been on Dwayne since he found the hand. The poor man's full of anxiety, he makes mistakes, is very forgetful. Paul told me that Dwayne has awful mood swings and I should consider carefully if I want the job."

"You accepted so you mustn't think working there will be a problem?" Juliet asked.

"I think it will go okay. At least, I hope so. I feel badly for Dwayne. He has to be on medication. Finding the hand has really messed him up."

Juliet made a face. "I imagine such a thing would make anyone anxious."

Shelly agreed and then said, "There's something about the situation with Dwayne that picks at me ... makes me uneasy."

"Maybe it's just the unknown," Juliet said. "A new job, new people, meeting new expectations."

"I'm not sure what it is." Shelly shifted the bag with the gift in it to her other hand.

Juliet glanced at her friend and pointedly asked, "Have you had any interesting dreams lately?"

Shelly sighed. "I haven't. Lauren hasn't been in any of my dreams."

"Too bad," Juliet said. "Jay told me there's an

immense amount of pressure on the department from nearly everyone in town to get this crime solved. This case sure could use some help."

Shelly didn't think she would be the help they needed.

10

Shelly sat at the beat-up wooden table in the small, cramped conference room in the police station with Jay sitting next to her and Abby Jackson's boyfriend, nineteen-year-old Adam Wall, sitting opposite them.

Jay had explained Shelly's presence by telling the young man that she was working in consultation with the police department. Despite the standup fan blowing on them, Shelly could feel little beads of sweat trickling down her back.

Jay had approached Shelly about sitting in on the interview with Adam asking her to attend in case the experience might trigger Shelly to have an important dream related to the proceedings.

Jay told her, "It's not that I'm a big proponent of the paranormal ... because I'm not, but you seem to have a heightened perception of situations and people around you and your dreams could be what happens when your subconscious works on a problem while you sleep. Your mind leads you towards something you only noticed in passing during the day. The importance of things gets high-lighted in your dreams. If you sit in on the interview, your subconscious might point you to things we overlook."

Jay made such a compelling case that Shelly couldn't think of an excuse not to attend the interview ... except that the idea terrified her and made her worry she wouldn't be able to help in any way.

On the table in front of Shelly, there was a note-book and a pen which she picked up to keep her hands from fidgeting. Feeling meek and like a fish out of water, she kept silent and listened to Jay's questions and the young man's answers.

Jay said, "Thanks for coming in again, Adam. I'd like to go over some of the things we talked about last time for clarification."

Adam Wall was about six feet tall, slender with the body of a long distance runner. His hair was sandy blond and his eyes were blue. He sat with his hands in his lap and a serious expression on his face. Shelly would have described his look as slightly defensive or arrogant and she wondered if she would look the same way if questioned by the police.

"Could you tell me again about the last time you saw Abby?" Jay opened a brown leather folder and glanced down at the papers inside of it.

Adam took a deep breath. "Abby and I had gone out. We hung out with a few friends down by the river, then some of us went out for something to eat. Abby and I drove around for a while and then she dropped me off at my house. I went inside and talked to my parents, then went up to my room."

"Did Abby plan on going right home?"

"Yes, she did."

"Did she say that to you?"

Adam said, "Yeah, she told me she was tired. She felt like a headache was coming on. It was pretty hot and humid that night. Abby got headaches sometimes when the weather was like that."

"You're going to college in the fall?"

"I'm going to Amherst. School starts at the end of August for freshmen."

"And Abby was also planning to go away to college?" Jay watched the young man's face.

"She was going to attend Boston College."

"What are you planning to study?" Jay questioned.

"Pre-med."

"What about Abby? What was she planning to study?"

"Abby was thinking of going to law school eventually, but she was having second thoughts and wasn't sure what she wanted for a career."

A sheen of sweat was visible on Adam's forehead and Shelly wondered if it was solely due to the heat or whether he was nervous and uncomfortable about the interview.

"Did Abby ever drop you at home after a night out and then go to meet someone else?"

Adam bit the inside of his cheek. "I don't know."

"She never talked about getting together with someone after you'd been out together?" Jay asked.

"I don't remember. Maybe she did." Adam shrugged. "I can't say for sure."

"I hear from some people that Abby may have wanted to break up before you both headed off to school," Jay noted. "Had you spoken about doing that?"

Adam's eyebrows seemed to move closer together. "We talked about it. We hadn't come to a decision yet."

"What were your thoughts? Did you feel strongly one way or the other?"

Adam shifted on the seat. "Sometimes I thought it would be a good idea to take a break from the relationship. Other times, I thought we should stay together and see how it worked out."

"Did you love Abby?"

Adam looked down at the tabletop. "Yeah." The word came out like a whisper.

"Was she in love with you?" Jay asked.

"I thought she was."

Jay asked in a gentle voice, "Do you have any idea who might have hurt Abby?"

Adam looked up and met Jay's eyes. "I don't have any idea."

"Had Abby mentioned an argument with anyone? Had she talked about not getting along with someone?"

Adam shook his head. "Things were normal."

Jay stood and made fleeting eye contact with Shelly. "I have to step out for a few minutes. I'll be right back."

When Jay exited the room, Shelly tried to make small talk with Adam. His answers were short and without any detail and in combination with his stiff posture, it was clear he had no interest in chatting.

Shelly said, "I heard Abby hurt her back. Do you know what caused her injury?"

Adam seemed surprised by the question. "Abby was running cross-country and she slipped on some loose rocks. She took a real bad fall. She was in the hospital for about a week."

"When did that happen?" Shelly asked.

"It was spring. April, maybe? She was on the school's spring cross-country team."

"Did she fully recover from the injury?"

"It still bothered her. She wasn't supposed to lift anything heavy for a while longer."

"Abby was working at the resort gift shop. How did she like the job?"

"She didn't," Adam said. "Abby liked to be outside, moving around. She didn't like being cooped up inside waiting on snooty customers." The young man's face clouded. "She didn't like the manager either."

"Why didn't she like him?"

"He was a jerk. Abby said he was too friendly. He made her uncomfortable."

"Did he do something to her?"

"No, nothing like that." Adam shook his head. "He was just a jerk, he made sexual comments and jokes, trying to be funny. Abby didn't like it. She missed working at the farm."

Shelly told Adam she had been hired to do some

baking for the farm. "Abby worked there for a few years, right?"

"All through high school. She liked working with the families and the kids. She loved the animals."

"Did she get along with the owners?"

"Oh, yeah. They seemed pretty good to work for. Dwayne, he owns the place with his sister, he runs it, too ... Abby said he was a good guy, cared about the farm animals, the employees. She said Dwayne was a little spacey sometimes, but overall she liked working at the farm and the orchard."

"What did she mean that Dwayne was spacey?" Shelly asked.

"Sort of lost in his thoughts, kind of forgetful sometimes, he would tell two different people to do the same job. Stuff like that."

The door opened and Jay walked back in and took her seat, apologizing again for being called away. "Adam, was there any indication that Abby might be seeing someone else?"

The young man sat up straight, a flash of anger in his eyes. A muscle twitched near his jaw. "No." His voice was loud and his cheeks reddened. "She wasn't seeing anyone but me."

Jay leaned back and attempted to move the inquiry into calmer waters. "If Abby went somewhere else after dropping you off at home that night, do you have any idea where she might have gone? To a friend's house? To get a late-night snack?"

Adam's face was still hard. "She wouldn't have done those things. If Abby was going to see a friend, she would have told me. She had a headache, she was going home."

"Did you ever go out after being dropped at home by Abby?" Jay asked.

Something darted over Adam's face and then was gone. "Once in a while."

"Did your parents always know when you went out late at night?"

Adam's eyes shifted around the room. "Not always. They'd be asleep. I'd get a text from a friend to go out for pizza or something. I didn't want to wake them so I just left."

"Did you leave them a note when you went out?"

"No." One of Adam's shoulders shrugged. "They wouldn't want me to go out late so I just went and came back. Anyway, I never stayed out long."

"Did you go out after Abby dropped you at home?" Jay questioned.

"No." Adam looked at Jay with an angry gaze. "I know what you're getting at. I was at home that whole night. I didn't see Abby again."

"We aren't accusing you of anything, Adam. We're only trying to figure out who was where, when. Occasionally, a person sees or hears something that doesn't seem important at the time, but might hold a small clue or could point us in a new direction. When we ask where people were and who they were with, it's only to create a timeline and to perhaps, stimulate that person's memory about some little thing."

Adam's posture relaxed slightly.

Jay asked in a calm, gentle voice. "Is there anything that you can remember about Abby's mood or maybe about something she said that now, under the circumstances, might be important or might shed some light on what happened to her?"

"Nothing. Nothing stands out. I don't know any more than what I've told you already. Twice." Adam glanced up at the wall clock and stood. "I have to get going."

Adam's tone and aggressive expression caused a shiver to run down Shelly's back.

The interview was over.

11

S helly and Juliet carried their homemade pizzas of tomato sauce, grilled Vidalia onions, diced peppers and mushrooms, and thin-sliced mozzarella to the patio and settled in their chairs while Justice rested in the grass nearby watching the birds, with one paw curled under her chest.

Shelly went on with her tale of trying out for the farm baking job by making two apple pies for Dwayne to try. "I was nervous even though I could make those pies in my sleep. Dwayne loved them and we signed a contract. The job is so flexible and the people working in the kitchen seem really nice."

"It sounds great. Congrats, again." Juliet eyed her friend. "If you ever make any extra pies, don't forget to bring one home, okay?"

Shelly chuckled. "There happens to be one for dessert tonight."

The young women chatted and ate and enjoyed the clear, pleasant breeze and mild temperatures. "Dwayne seems nice," Shelly said. "But the nephew, Paul, he does the marketing for the farm, voiced his concerns about Dwayne's mental health."

"The poor guy suffered a shock when he found the hand. It might take some time for him to deal with all of that." Juliet sipped her iced tea with lemonade.

"Dwayne is taking medication for anxiety. Paul told me his uncle is forgetful and makes mistakes. He seemed very worried."

"How was Dwayne when you talked to him?"

Shelly said, "He was fine. He gave me a tour, showed me the kitchen, answered all of my questions. He was nice, friendly. I wouldn't have suspected he was dealing with anxiety."

"Dwayne probably just needs some time," Juliet said. "Now tell me about sitting in with Jay during Adam Wall's interview."

Shelly gave her the summarized version of the meeting and then said, "I didn't know what to think about Adam. Sometimes he seemed to be holding back information. He's a young guy who just lost his girlfriend. He must be torn up about it, but he didn't show much emotion at all. He seemed very defensive and angry. At one point, he snapped at Jay and raised his voice. I kept thinking about what the woman on the woodland hike told me about overhearing some women talk about Adam ... that he was controlling with Abby and he told her she couldn't be with anyone else. That was in the back of my mind and I bet it colored my feelings about Adam."

"Did anything important come out of the interview?" Juliet wiped at the corner of her mouth with a napkin.

"Nothing stunning," Shelly said. "Adam did admit he sometimes would leave the house late at night while his parents were sleeping to go meet a friend, but he was adamant that he stayed at home after Abby left him off."

"Did he say anything about the possibility they might break up before leaving for college? Did they discuss it?"

A long string of mozzarella stretched from the pizza slice Shelly was holding all the way to her mouth. She pinched it so it broke apart. "He said they had talked about it and were still on the fence about what to do. He said he loved Abby."

"I wonder," Juliet pondered. "We've heard through the grapevine that Adam said some harsh things to Abby when she talked about breaking up with him. It makes me wonder about the guy. I don't like the things I've heard."

Shelly said, "We have to remember those things might only be hearsay. It might be gossip with no basis in fact."

"I think it would be good to talk to one of Abby's girlfriends. See what Abby thought about Adam. She and a good friend must have talked about such things."

"Adam also mentioned that the manager of the gift shop where Abby worked was a real pest saying off-color things to Abby, making sexual jokes. She didn't like it and she didn't like the man either. Adam said Abby told him she was uncomfortable around the manager."

"No wonder," Juliet sighed and rolled her eyes. "Why do some guys think women want to hear their stupid comments and jokes. Be normal, not like some leering goon. Gosh."

Justice jumped up on Shelly's lap and begin to purr. "I think the store manager needs to be looked at by the police. That friend we met at the pub a few days ago told us the manager touched

Abby inappropriately. I have suspicions about him."

"That's smart. Did you tell Jay what we heard?"

"I did. Have you seen her lately?"

"No." Juliet shook her head. "She's straight out working all kinds of crazy hours on this thing."

"She looked tired at the interview. Maybe we should make dinner for her sometime and drop it off at the house."

Juliet agreed it was a good idea.

Shelly brought up something else. "I asked Adam about Abby's back injury. Remember the gift shop manager told me Abby got hurt and couldn't work at the farm anymore. That's how she ended up working at the gift shop this summer. Adam said Abby was on the cross country team at school. She was doing a training run in the woods and she fell and hurt her back. Adam didn't seem to have any worries about the injury. Something about the way he talked about it made me uneasy."

"Like how? What did he say?"

"It wasn't really what he said. It was more how he talked about it, sort of nonchalant, it was no big deal, he was emotionless. Abby was in the hospital for almost a week. It must have been a big deal. He spoke about it as if it was nothing. She must have been in pain, upset. It didn't seem to faze him one bit."

"Adam doesn't seem to be earning many points in the 'good guy' column," Juliet said with a tone of disgust.

"He came across as sort of selfish and self-absorbed," Shelly explained.

"Is his behavior enough for us to be suspicious of him?" Juliet tilted her head to the side in question.

"I sure think it is, but Jay is the one who makes those decisions." Shelly gave a shrug. "It's my opinion based on his answers to questions and some gossip we've heard. Those are pretty slim reasons to think he might be guilty of killing Abby."

"Feelings and intuition should never be discounted," Juliet said. "It's all enough to keep Adam on the suspect list." After sitting and finishing their pizzas, Juliet asked, "Have you had any interesting dreams lately?"

Letting out a slight groan, Shelly shook her head. "I haven't. I can't even remember any of them. Maybe I've stopped dreaming."

Juliet smiled. "You haven't. Most people don't recall their dreams. We all dream, they just don't stick with us most of the time."

"I wish I could do more to help Jay. She seems to

think I have some special skill where I can pick up things from situations and people." Shelly frowned. "I can't."

"I think you're wrong about that. You're one of the most intuitive people I know. You seem to be able to read people. You're very sensitive to other people's feelings."

Shelly sighed. "Well, it isn't anything that's going to help the police. They should hire a real psychic."

"I don't think that's in Jay's budget." Juliet let out a chuckle. "I also don't think that would be something they could bring to the town meeting for a vote."

"Too bad." Shelly put her chin in her hand. "Because I'm not going to be of any help."

"It's not over yet." Juliet stood up to clear away the dinner plates. "It's time for dessert and someone promised me apple pie."

"Oh, I forgot," Shelly joked. "I left it at the farm."

"Then we'll just have to drive on over there and get it."

With the cat following after them, the young women went inside, cleaned up the dishes, and took slices of warm apple pie with ice cream to the living room and sat on the sofa with Justice snuggling in between them.

"Where could Abby's car be?" Juliet asked out of the blue. "How could it disappear into thin air?"

Shelly's index finger had a bit of ice cream on it so she offered it to the Calico who gently licked off every drop making sure the finger was clean. "I have no idea, unless it's been hidden in someone's garage or barn or outbuilding. If it was out in the open, someone would have seen it by now."

Juliet speculated. "I guess it could be in a public parking garage in some city, but I don't think it could have gotten far from here without an officer from another town spotting it."

"You're probably right although the alert about the car didn't go out for about twelve hours after Abby disappeared," Shelly said. "Twelve hours of driving could have taken the car a very long way."

"You're right." Juliet's shoulders slumped and she released a defeated sigh. "It's long gone and probably never to be found."

Shelly said hopefully, "If the car went through toll plazas, there would be a video or photographic record of it passing by and the police will know which way it was headed."

Juliet shook her head. "Do you think the killer would be dumb enough to travel on a toll highway?

He must know they photo every car that travels through."

"We can hope." The corners of Shelly's lip turned up as she reached over to stroke the sleeping cat's fur. "The more important question is where is Abby's body?"

"With the car?" Juliet asked.

"I don't know, but I would guess not," Shelly said. "It would be too risky to travel far with a body in the car, even in the trunk. My guess is that the killer left the body someplace around here and then drove the car away to hide it." A thought flickered in Shelly's brain and then, in a fleeting second, it was gone.

Or are the body and the car hidden here in Paxton Park?

12

The scent of cinnamon and apples drifted on the air in the corner of the farm's huge kitchen where Shelly worked on her first batch of pies while the other workers buzzed around completing their own tasks. It was late afternoon and Shelly went straight to the farm after finishing up her job at the diner. After placing six pies in the commercial ovens, she stepped outside for a few minutes to sit at the picnic table before working on the last batch.

The sky was a bright, clear blue with an occasional wispy cloud showing high in the atmosphere. Shelly sipped from the glass of water she'd taken outside and then she put her hands over her head and stretched her back from side to side.

"Too much baking in one day?" Dwayne

approached the picnic table wearing jeans, a long-sleeved shirt despite the heat, and his baseball cap and he sat down opposite Shelly.

"My back gets stiff no matter what I do," she told the older man.

"Mine should get stiff, but it doesn't. It should have given out by now, but nope, it keeps on going without a problem. I suppose I'll have to keep working until the old back gives up." Dwayne smiled at the young woman.

"It seems that will be a very long time from now." Shelly returned the smile.

Dwayne asked her questions about her job at the diner, about living in Boston, about the car accident that claimed her sister's life, and how she was faring in her move to the resort town. Shelly answered the questions thoughtfully and the two discussed the pros and cons of living in the city versus the country before moving the conversation to loss and how to handle grief.

"I lost my wife and son to a car accident fifteen years ago," Dwayne said. "I thought my heart had shattered into a million pieces and would never be whole again."

"Is it whole now?" Shelly asked.

"It is not and it never will be again." Dwayne

took off his hat and placed it on the table. "I'm sorry to say that to you while your grief is so new, but don't despair. When you love someone and lose them, the heart breaks and is never the same, but you can still go on, find love, enjoy life, be active, and happy. You're just not the same as you were before."

"Are you happy?" Shelly asked.

Dwayne said, "I was happy until I found Abby's hand. That brought up all my old heartbreak. I lost my family to an accident. Abby lost her life to a monster who stole it from her. It makes me angry, very angry ... and terribly sad."

"I understand Abby worked here on the farm. I heard she loved it."

"That girl was a ray of sunlight. She loved working hard, loved the animals and taking care of them. Abby was a naturally happy person, friendly, helpful, kind. She was good with all the people who visited here from the oldest ones all the way down to the little babies."

A smile spread over Shelly's face as she listened to Dwayne sing Abby's praises.

"Why can't the police find her body?" Dwayne asked. "Isn't there any evidence to follow?"

Shelly and Dwayne turned their heads when they heard the laugh of a young child. The little boy and his parents had walked past a stack of hay into the petting zoo where a goat nuzzled the child on the belly. The giggles rang in the air like little cymbals.

"Sweet kid." Dwayne scratched his chin and sighed. "I guess I'm not being fair to the police. Trying to find the body and the killer must be like looking for a needle in a haystack."

Shelly agreed and she and Dwayne talked for a few more minutes until a young woman around eighteen with long brown hair and big brown eyes came over to the table with a message for the older man. "Lizzie says you're supposed to be at the office to meet the construction man. He's there waiting for you."

"Oh, dang it. I forgot all about it." Dwayne pushed himself up, said goodbye to Shelly, and hurried past the food barn towards the office located in the log cabin.

Shelly watched him go thinking about how his nephew, Paul, had told her that Dwayne was becoming more and more forgetful. Checking her phone for the time, she saw she had five more minutes before the pies needed to be checked. Realizing the dark-haired girl was still standing next to the table, Shelly looked up. "Do you want to sit down?"

The slim brunette nervously slid over the bench.

Shelly introduced herself and the young woman said, "I'm Dana."

She looked at Shelly, but didn't say anything else.

"You work here at the farm?" Shelly asked to start a conversation.

Dana nodded. "Depending on the day, I'm either working in the food barn, the petting zoo, selling tickets to pick apples in the orchard, or working in the orchard or at the corn maze."

"You do it all," Shelly said with a smile.

"I heard you and Dwayne talking about Abby."

"You must have known her," Shelly said. "From working here."

"Yeah, and we were in school together and on the cross country running team."

"Were you friends?"

"Not best friends, but friends," Dana said. "We didn't really hang out together outside of school, the team, and work."

"I'm sorry about the loss," Shelly said.

Dana looked down at her hands. "I was running on the trails one day after school. It wasn't a scheduled training. I was running on my own. Most of us put in extra training hours outside of the workouts with the team. There's a six-mile path that winds around the base of the mountain ... one part goes right past the resort."

Shelly couldn't imagine why Dana was telling her this.

"It's a good training run. We all know about it. We all use it."

Waiting for the girl to go on, Shelly kept quiet.

"Anyway, this particular day, I started to feel sick while I was running so I stopped and walked off the trail and climbed up to a flat rock where I rested. I almost fell asleep in the sun until I heard footsteps and I looked around expecting a runner from our team to go past."

"Who was it?"

"It wasn't anyone from the team. It was Abby's boyfriend, Adam. I watched him for a while. He stood by a tree next to the trail. He didn't know I was there."

"What happened?" Shelly's heart started to race.

"Abby came running along and Adam stepped out. Abby looked really surprised to see him. They talked, but I couldn't make out what they were saying. Adam got angry, his voice got loud. He started to fight with Abby. He pushed her hard and Abby almost fell. She caught herself and came up to

Adam and hit him across the face. Adam screamed and punched Abby in the face. She staggered back. She fell backwards and tumbled down the ravine next to the trail. She screamed as she fell." Dana's breathing was shallow and fast.

"Adam pushed her down the ravine?" Shelly couldn't believe her ears.

"That's what happened to Abby. She hurt her back because of Adam. She was in the hospital."

"When Abby fell, what did you do?"

"I came off the rock and went down the hill. Adam didn't see me. I started to run towards him like I had just shown up. I acted like I hadn't seen what happened. I asked what was wrong. He told me Abby had been running and she slipped on the stones and fell down the hill. I told him to call "911" and I ran down to help Abby. She had passed out. I stayed with her until help came." Dana moved her hand over her eyes and Shelly could see her fingers shaking.

"How did Adam explain being on the trails if Abby was out for a run?" Shelly asked.

"I asked him at the hospital why he was in the woods. He told me he was going to take pictures of Abby as she ran by." Dana's chin jutted out. "That's not why he was there."

"Why do you think he was there?" Shelly asked.

"I think he wanted to talk to Abby in private. We all knew Abby ran the trails that day of the week. Adam knew she'd run by him on that path."

"Do you think he wanted to hurt Abby?" Shelly could feel the sweat beading on the back of her neck.

"I don't know what he was doing."

"Have you told anyone about this?" Shelly asked.

"No." Dana looked like she was about to cry.

"Why did you tell me?" Shelly didn't understand why Dana would tell a stranger her story.

"I heard you and Dwayne talking. You seem nice. I need someone to tell me what they think. I can't tell my family or my friends what happened. I don't want it to sound like I'm accusing Adam of anything. I need advice." Tears began streaming down the young woman's face.

Shelly reached across the table and took the girl's hand. "I think you should go talk to the police."

A look of horror covered Dana's face.

"It's okay. My friend's sister is a police officer in town. Go talk to her. Her name is Jayne Landers-Smyth. You'll like her. She's easy to talk to. Tell her what you just told me, then it will be in the hands of the police and you won't have to think about it anymore."

"Okay." Dana nodded and brushed the tears from her cheeks. "That sounds like a good idea."

"It's the right thing to do. And Jayne will keep what you tell her in confidence. No one will know you talked to her."

A look of relief washed over Dana's face. "Okay. I didn't know I could be anonymous. That makes me feel better." Swallowing hard, the young woman looked at Shelly. "Do you think Adam killed Abby?"

Before Shelly could give an answer, someone from the kitchen stepped out of the food barn and glanced around until she noticed Shelly at the picnic table. "Shelly. The oven timer went off a minute ago. You want me to take the pies out?"

"Oh. Thanks." Shelly stood up and before hurrying off to the barn, she told Dana, "I'll be here for another two hours today if you need to talk."

With her head pounding from what Dana had told her, Shelly ran inside to rescue the pies.

13

J ack returned from leading the adventure
trip and immediately made plans to meet
Shelly and spend the day with her. In the
morning, they biked the easier paths
around the mountain so Shelly wouldn't have to deal
with too many hills. The injuries from the attack on
her from the last murder case had pretty much
healed and already she felt like she could tackle
more strenuous exercise. Rushing along under the
dappled sunlight, past the towering pines, with the
warm wind on her face, Shelly's heart swelled with
joy as she and Jack pedaled their bicycles over the
trails.

When they finished the twelve-mile ride, the
couple stopped at the resort's Mountain Pub for
lunch. The pub was built in post and beam style

with a cathedral ceiling and warm, deep golden wood on the walls, floor, and ceiling promoting a rustic, cozy atmosphere. Big windows faced the mountains affording beautiful views of the pines, fields, mountain, and lake.

Sitting by the window, Shelly and Jack ordered drinks and shared an appetizer while she gave him a rundown on all he'd missed during the week.

"Why did Jay want you to sit in on the interview with Adam Wall?" Jack asked, not knowing about Shelly's meaningful dreams and confused as to how she could be of any help to law enforcement.

Before answering, Shelly took a swallow of her beverage in order to gather her thoughts and consider how to respond. "Jay thinks I have a strong intuition, that I pick up on subtle things about people and situations that most people miss. I don't know that I agree with her, but she asked and I felt obligated to help, so I went."

"Interesting." Jack looked at the young woman across from him, his blue eyes like lasers on her. "There were people in the military like that. They had an uncanny ability to anticipate danger. Some men and women can do that sort of thing naturally, it is part of who they are. For some reason, they're more skilled at noticing and reading subtle signals that others give off. I found it fascinating." He leaned forward. "When something's wrong, is there some tiny scent on the air that more intuitive people can pick up on? Is there a vibration in the air that doesn't seem normal? Is there a heightened sense of sight or hearing that sets off an alarm in the person's brain? I talked to some of the men who seemed to have this skill. They told me they had no idea what was alerting them to the danger, somehow they just knew it was coming."

Shelly listened with focused attention, intrigued by Jack's experience with the soldiers who could perceive danger and with his questions and speculation about how people were able to sense such things. Did the military have an understanding of these skills? She'd bet there weren't any soldiers who had dream premonitions ... or were there?

When Jack asked Shelly a question, she didn't hear what he said because she was deep in thought about their conversation, so Jack had to repeat it. "Have you always been so intuitive?"

Shelly shook herself out of her thoughts. "No." Sadness pulled at her mouth and she answered softly. "It all seemed to start after the accident."

Jack reached across the table and held Shelly's

hand. "What you're able to sense about others could be very helpful to people."

A smile spread over Shelly's face and she held tighter to Jack's hand. "You're a very kind man, Jack Graham."

The two stared into each other's eyes for almost a minute.

With a smile, Jack said, "Can your senses pick up on what I'm feeling?"

With a sparkle in her eyes, Shelly tilted her head and leaned closer. "I think they can."

The flirting was interrupted when the waiter came over with the lunch orders and set the plates down in front of the two romantics. After enjoying the food, Shelly and Jack rode their bikes into town and strolled hand in hand along the brick sidewalks window shopping and then they watched the tourists while sitting on a bench in the town common eating ice cream cones.

"This has been the best day," Jack announced as he and Shelly parked the bikes behind her house and went inside, greeted Justice, poured glasses of lemonade, and headed to the front porch to sit in the rockers. The cat jumped up on Jack's lap and settled down expecting a few scratches under her cheeks.

Shelly let out a laugh at the feline's behavior. "I think you have a fan."

Jack looked down at the sweet little animal. "I'm glad. The feeling is mutual," he said as he accommodated Justice's desire to be patted.

"Tell me more about your new job," Jack said rocking slowly back and forth in the chair being careful not to tip the cat.

After giving him details about the temporary baking position, Shelly brought up the conversation she had with Paul, Dwayne's nephew. "Paul thinks Dwayne should retire. He says the man is making mistakes and is very forgetful."

"Dwayne hasn't had it easy. He lost his wife and son, he had the misfortune to find Abby's hand, and he's worked hard on the farm for years. Maybe it's time for him to relax."

"I get the impression that Dwayne loves that farm. I think he'd be lost without the work. From listening to him talk, I think it gives him a sense of stability and purpose. It might not be good for him to retire." Shelly watched the ice cubes floating in her glass. "I can't help thinking that Paul has an ulterior motive for hoping Dwayne might retire."

Jack narrowed his eyes. "You think he wants to take over the place?"

"Maybe I'm being suspicious," Shelly said. "Since Paul's mother owns half of the farm, wouldn't Paul eventually inherit her half? And if Dwayne's only living relatives are Paul and his mother, wouldn't Paul inherit the whole farm one day? Why would he be so keen on having Dwayne retire?"

Jack said, "Dwayne really might be becoming incapable of handling the operation of the place ... or his ideas about how to run the farm might clash with Paul's more modern views. It's not easy to keep a big farm like that going, it's very expensive. It's often necessary to expand into different things like they've done by adding the brewery, the food barn, the animals, the fall activities. It draws in a lot of paying customers. Maybe Dwayne is hindering some of Paul's plans. Paul may feel Dwayne's ideas are no longer in the business's best interests."

"I didn't think of it that way. Maybe you're right." Shelly steered the conversation to lighter topics. With Jack beside her, she wanted to forget the recent troubles that had happened in town, if only for a few hours.

The two made dinner together and watched a movie, snuggling on the sofa with Justice pushing her way in between them. Jack had to head home when the film finished since he had to be at the mountain at 6am the next day. Shelly walked him to the door, but before descending the steps, he pulled the young woman into a tight hug and they shared a long, passionate kiss under the porch light. Breathless and with her cheeks flushed pink, Shelly waved and watched as Jack pedaled away down the lane.

After locking the front door and putting some glasses into the dishwasher, Shelly yawned and stretched, suddenly feeling exhausted from all the outdoor activities she'd done with Jack. With the cat padding after her, she headed for the bedroom, changed, and slipped under the covers to read before falling asleep.

Justice curled up beside her owner and began to purr and every few minutes, Shelly's head would fall forward and snap up as she drifted into sleep and then woke with a start. Giving up on the book, she set it on the side table, turned out the light, and burrowed under the blanket feeling content and happy.

Falling into a deep sleep, Shelly began to dream.

She ran and ran through the forest, with her heart pounding and panic rushing through her veins. A strong wind blew against her impeding her progress. She had to hurry or it would be too late.

Emerging from the woods into an open field, Shelly saw trees down and a building leveled.

Lauren stepped out from behind the rubble and lifted her arms reaching for her sister, and like in the last dream she remembered, Lauren's hands were missing.

Trying to reach her, Shelly climbed over the trees and plodded clumsily towards her sister with legs so heavy she could barely move them. She fell and stood up and fell again. Tears streamed down her face. *Lauren.*

With her handless arms hanging by her sides, Lauren watched with a sad, lonely expression as Shelly fell once more and began to crawl on hands and knees desperate to get to her.

Lauren shook her head slowly from side to side and then turned and stumbled back behind the rubble.

Shelly shrieked for Lauren to wait. *Wait for me. I'm coming.* But her sister disappeared from view and Shelly collapsed, sobbing, onto the muddy ground.

When she lifted her face, her vision began to spin, faster and faster, and she dug her fingers into the wet soil trying to stop the motion. In a moment, she was high in the air looking down towards the ground.

A dark car twirled crazily in the air, suspended high above the land, rotating and rotating.

It began to fall ... down it plummeted ... the car tumbled, down, down, deep into the earth ... and then it was gone.

Too late.

14

After her workday at the diner was done, Shelly walked along the trails that hugged the lower part of the mountain admiring the pine trees rising all around like sentries there to protect her. Her leg was sore and her limp was more pronounced from all the biking she'd done with Jack the day before, but she wanted to be outside in the quiet of the woods to have a chance to think and clear her head of the disturbing dream she'd had the night before.

Aware that she needed to be careful in the forest alone, Shelly selected the trail she was walking on because of its usual traffic of cyclists, runners, and hikers and she carried a canister of pepper spray in one hand and her phone in the other.

Images from the dream had popped into her

head all day while she baked in the kitchen of the diner. If Juliet and Jay hadn't talked to her about precognition and people whose dreams warned of coming events and gave clues to crimes, she would have brushed the nightmare off and wouldn't have let it bother her. Knowing now that her nighttime visions, at least the ones with Lauren in them, might be trying to tell her something, the disturbing aspects of last night's dream got under her skin and stayed there.

Although she knew she would have to speak to Jay about it eventually, the thought of sharing the details with anyone made her feel ill.

Shelly headed down a small gravelly path that led to the lake where she sat on a big rock at the edge and watched kayakers glide easily over the clear, blue water. On the opposite shore, people jumped in from rope swings, others played at the edge with little children, and a few swam with practiced strokes across the middle of the lake.

A rusting noise behind her made Shelly's heart jump and she turned to see what it was. A man in his early sixties wearing long shorts, a t-shirt, and a baseball hat strolled down towards the water with a black Labrador at his side. The dog spotted Shelly on the rock and trotted over to greet her.

The Lab's friendly demeanor made her chuckle as it pushed its nose against her hand asking for a pat.

"That's Buddy, the world's friendliest animal." The man nodded to her.

"He's great." Shelly scratched the dog behind the ears and he gave her a lick on the hand with his long, pink tongue.

The man called to the dog and threw a sick into the water and when the dog saw their game had started, he ran and jumped into the lake and swam for the stick.

"It's our daily routine," the man told Shelly. "We take our walk and then come to the lake for a few stick retrievals."

Shelly asked some questions about the dog and the man was happy to tell her all about his four-legged companion.

"Do you live around here or just visiting?" the man asked.

"I moved to town a few months ago. I work in the diner as a baker supplying the diner and the resort's bakery with goods."

The man asked about her background and Shelly told him about living in Boston, being in an accident ... but leaving out many of the details ... and how she decided to make a change and move to the mountain to accept a new job.

"How do you like it so far?"

"I like it very much. I've made some friends and I love all the outdoor activities and being near the lake and the trails."

"Do you ski?" the man asked.

"I do, although not very well." Shelly smiled.

"You'll get better being able to practice all the time. You know you get free skiing as part of your compensation for being a resort employee?"

Shelly nodded. "I remember seeing that in the contract. Do you work for the resort?"

"I did. I worked as an accountant for over twenty years. I recently took early retirement, only been out for a few weeks ... we thought about moving to some place new, but quickly tossed that idea. We like it here."

"Are you adjusting to retirement well?" Shelly asked.

The man's face clouded. "I'm growing used to it."

"Miss your job?"

"It's not that. I'm happy to be done with going to an office all day, but...." the man let his voice trail off.

Shelly tilted her head in question. "But, you have some reservations?"

The dog galloped out of the water, dropped the stick, and shook the droplets from his fur with a vigorous shake of his body. The man jumped back to avoid getting wet, then leaned forward to pick up the stick and toss it into the lake. He walked over to where Shelly sat on the rock. "Mind if I sit?"

She nodded and scrooted over to make room.

"I was enjoying the freedom of being out of the workplace. Not long ago, Buddy and I were out for a walk." The man paused. "Buddy made a gruesome discovery."

Shelly turned with wide eyes and asked with a gentle tone. "Buddy was the dog that found the hand?"

The man gave a nod. "He barked and barked. He ran at me and then rushed to the spot where he found it, back and forth until I went over to see what had grabbed his attention. I almost passed out when I saw what it was."

Shelly couldn't suppress a shudder.

"I knew the girl, Abby Jackson. She was a good kid." The man passed his hand over his face.

"How did you know her?" Shelly asked.

"Our families were friendly," he said. "We knew each other from the kids' sports. Our daughter was a year older than Abby. They both ran cross-country, played on the soccer team. I was pretty sure that the discovery Buddy made belonged to Abby. My wife and I were horrified and heartbroken. Our daughter attends college in Boston. We drove down to tell her … tell her that Abby must be dead."

"I'm so sorry," Shelly told the man.

"If it wasn't for the dog, I don't think I'd ever walk in the woods again. Sometimes when we're walking and Buddy gets excited over something or starts sniffing something, I experience a panic attack. It passes. I love the mountains and the forest. I'm going to keep walking every day. I'm determined to over-come my stress and anxiety."

Shelly praised the man and encouraged him to continue his walks. "I'm glad you won't allow the killer to steal away your love of your home."

"How I wish the police would solve this mystery and find Abby." The dog carried the stick to the man and he threw it.

"Have you talked to Abby's parents?" Shelly asked.

The man sighed. "Yes. My wife and I visited with them not long ago."

"Do they have suspicions about who might have done this?" Shelly wondered if the family could even think straight under the circumstances.

"They don't. Sandra and Ben, Abby's parents, don't know what to think. Their guess is that it was random."

"Do you think it was random?" Shelly asked.

"I know Sandra and Ben don't want to think that a killer is living here in town with all of us. They prefer to see the evil as an outside force. I hope it was random, but my feeling is that the person who did this walks among us."

A chill rushed over Shelly's skin as the possibility raced through her mind that this man might be the one who killed Abby and hid her body. Reaching into her pocket, she gripped the pepper spray she'd slipped there when she sat down on the rock. Swallowing hard to clear her throat, Shelly asked, "You think the killer lives in town?"

"I don't know, it's only a feeling I have. It seems to me the attacker must have known Abby."

Shelly's momentary flash of panic that she might be sitting next to a killer began to subside. "What makes you think so?"

The dog came out of the water, dropped the stick, and began to sniff around the trees.

"The locations of the terrible finds make me think so. Buddy and I found one of the hands near the trail Abby often trained on. Poor Dwayne

Thomas, the guy that owns Glad Hill Farm and the orchard, he found the other one. Abby worked at that farm for years. She loved that farm. It seems like the killer knew her. It couldn't be random. The two places were important to Abby. The killer seems to be thumbing his nose at all of us."

What the man had just pointed out had never occurred to Shelly and she hoped the police had made the link that the killer left Abby's hands at two places that were important to her. "That makes a lot of sense. I bet you're right. Did you mention this to the police?"

"I brought it up, yes."

"Is there anyone you can think of who would do such a thing?" Shelly asked.

"I have no idea ... and honestly, I hope I don't know the person responsible. How could a person hide what a monster they really are?" The man shook his head. "I hope I haven't been tricked for years by the killer ... all the while him pretending to be a normal person and me never picking up that a monster lurked within."

The man's words caused a prickly sensation to scratch at Shelly's skin.

The man moved a little on the rock so he could

face Shelly. "Are you surprised I'm telling you all of this?"

"A little," she admitted.

Shifting his gaze out over the lake, he said, "Sometimes it's easier to talk to a stranger about such things. I don't like to keep repeating things about the incident over and over to my wife or to my friends. I know they're upset enough, and me jabbering on about it all would only make them feel worse." The man shrugged one of his shoulders. "Thanks for listening to me."

Shelly understood his sentiments. She felt the same way about the car accident and about how much she missed Lauren. Sometimes it was easier to talk to someone who wasn't so closely involved with your pain ... sometimes it was easier to jabber at someone who would lend a sympathetic ear and then walk away, unburdened by your blubbering.

Shelly gave the man's arm a pat and then, with a heavy sigh, she joined him in staring out over the still, peaceful blue lake.

15

Shelly, Juliet, and Jay, still wearing her police uniform, sat around the small table in the screened room at the back of Juliet's cottage sipping glasses of sparkling fruit juice. The ceiling fan circled lazily overhead cooling the space.

Jay suggested they meet at Juliet's place instead of at a café or restaurant because everywhere she went, people would come up to her either to offer advice for the investigation or to demand the police find the killer.

Justice had come along to the gathering, too, and was resting on the back of an easy chair looking out into the yard watching the birds fly in and out of the trees and the squirrels and chipmunks scurry over the grass. When a bird flew close by the screen,

Justice would crouch in a hunting position and make little clicking sounds until the bird disappeared.

"I had another dream," Shelly announced trying not to let the alarm she felt show in her voice.

Juliet's hand froze in the air holding the carafe of juice and she shifted her eyes to her friend.

Jay swallowed the bite of cookie, placed the rest of it on her dessert plate, and cleared her throat. Keeping her tone even, she asked, "When?"

"Two nights ago."

"You didn't tell me," Juliet said with a frown.

"It upset me. I had to think about it for a while before telling anyone."

"Was Lauren in it?" Juliet asked.

As Shelly gave the tiniest of nods, Justice let out a low growl.

"Can you tell us about it?" Jay asked.

Shelly swallowed hard and then reported the details of the dream, trying carefully to remember everything she saw and heard, and everything she felt. "And then the car fell into the earth and was gone."

"Well," Jay said.

"I can see why it was upsetting." Juliet shifted around on her seat and nervously pushed a lock of her hair from her face. "Why didn't Lauren wait for you? You were trying to help her." Juliet moaned. "That was a stupid question. I know it was just a dream."

"I couldn't get to her." With her elbow on the table, Shelly rested her chin in her hand. "I tried and tried."

Jay said, "Can you describe the landscape again?"

Shelly looked across the table at the police officer. "It seemed like a storm had gone through the area. Some trees were down, a building had collapsed, the ground was muddy."

"Were there any sounds?" Jay asked.

Shelly though about that. "No, only the wind."

"What did it sound like?" Jay asked. "A storm kind of wind? A breezy day? A hurricane?"

"A breezy day."

"Were any other people around?"

"No one. Just me. And Lauren." Emotion hit Shelly unexpectedly and she had to blink back some tears.

"The car appeared out of nowhere?" Jay asked.

"That's right. All of a sudden, I was in the air watching the car rotating slightly below me."

"Was anyone in the car as it twirled?" Juliet asked.

"I'm not sure. I couldn't see through the windows."

Jay nodded. "Could you hear any voices?"

"No voices. Just the breeze."

"Did you recognize where you were?" Jay questioned.

"No. Really, it could have been any place."

"Were there other buildings around? Any houses?"

"Nothing else. Just the knocked down building." Shelly groaned. "This isn't any help at all."

"It is helpful," Jay said kindly. "We need to think about the clues your brain is trying to send you. We need to analyze the information. It takes time."

"Lauren was in the dream," Juliet said. "So it means something. We'll figure it out."

"Can you describe the car?" Jay asked.

"It was a dark-colored car. I couldn't see through the windows. It was twirling in the air, and then it started to spin faster."

"Can you remember anything else about it? Could you see it clearly?" Jay asked.

Shelly put her hands over her eyes trying to block out the things in the room so she could focus on recalling the details of the dream. After a half-minute, she dropped her hands. "I think it was black.

It looked like a small SUV, maybe a Honda." Shelly nodded. "I think I saw the "H" near the front grill and on the back under the window. I think it was a Honda-CRV."

One of Jay's eyebrows went up. "A Honda-CRV? Black?"

"Yeah," Shelly said. "You know the kind of car? It's a small SUV."

"I know it," Jay said softly.

Juliet sat up to attention. "What kind of a car did Abby drive?"

Jay took a sip from her glass. "A Honda-CRV."

Juliet's eyes flashed with excitement. "Was her car black?"

"It was."

Shelly's face seemed to pale, but she tried to dismiss the fact in her dream. "I must have heard that on the news reports when Abby disappeared. I must have heard the make and model and color of her car. That must be why I dreamt that particular vehicle. Yes, that explains it." A light sheen of sweat showed on Shelly's forehead.

Jay wasn't so sure that was the explanation. "What happened to the car again?"

"It was suspended in the air," Shelly said. "It was spinning, rotating. Then it fell like someone snipped the string that was holding it in the air. The car fell, it hit the earth, and then it was gone."

"Did you hear anything as it fell?" Jay asked.

"No. I didn't hear it crash when it hit the ground, there wasn't any sound at all. Maybe only a thud."

"Did it fall into a hole?" Jay asked.

"It was like a dark pit," Shelly told Jay.

"And what did you feel from Lauren?"

"Hopelessness, loneliness, she had given up." Sadness crept over Shelly's face as she gripped her hands together. She didn't want to talk about the dream anymore. "I went for a walk in the woods today after work."

"Alone?" Juliet almost shouted. "I don't think that's a good idea."

Shelly explained the well-traveled route she took and that she carried pepper spray with her.

"I still don't think it's a good idea to walk alone." Juliet looked at her sister to back her up.

"You might not want to walk alone in the woods," Jay said. "Maybe walk around town instead. You know, until the killer is caught."

Shelly didn't respond to the suggestions. "I met a man in the woods, by the lake. I was sitting on a rock watching the people swimming and kayaking."

"What happened?" Juliet sounded alarmed.

"Nothing. We talked." Shelly let out a long sigh. "It turns out that the man was the one who found the hand, the first hand, when he was walking in the woods with his dog."

"What did he say?" Jay asked.

"Probably what he told you. He said he told the police what he had been thinking."

"What had he been thinking?" Juliet asked.

"He thinks the killer lives in town or at least, nearby," Shelly said. "He doesn't think it was random because of the locations where the hands were placed."

"What does that mean?" Juliet asked, her face clouded by confusion.

"He means," Jay said. "That the hands were found in places that were important to Abby."

"Why would the killer do that?" Juliet asked.

"Good question," Shelly said.

Jay said, "Sometimes, a criminal will do things like that as a display of power. At times, it is done to taunt the police. Other times, it is meant to humble the victim, to put them in their place. The killer puts an item in places that meant something to the victim as a final insult to the person ... the message being, *I know you liked this place, but you'll never enjoy it again.* It's a power trip."

"Monster," Juliet whispered.

Shelly said, "I think the man is right. The killer must live in town. How else would he know enough about Abby to mark two places that were important to her?"

"It's possible," Jay said.

Shelly and Juliet both knew Jay's comment was deliberately vague as she was unable to divulge much of anything about the on-going investigation.

"Do you have any suspects?" Shelly asked.

"We have people we're taking closer looks at." Jay nodded.

Juliet said, "That is double-speak meaning you don't have a suspect."

"We're tracking down every clue."

Juliet dropped her chin, but lifted her eyes to stare at her sister. "I know the drill, Jay. You can't tell us anything. You don't need to give us those canned lines you use with the press."

"Sorry. It's habit. I can't tell you anything ... except that I'd sure like to find something, anything that could point us in the right direction."

"Abby's family must be sick, and bewildered, and angry," Shelly noted.

"First of all, they want their daughter back." Jay had to pause before going on. "They know she's dead. They just want to give her a proper burial. And then, they want us to find her killer." Jay looked Shelly in the eye. "I'm interviewing the parents again tomorrow afternoon. Would you sit in again like you did when I talked to Abby's boyfriend?"

A wave of nervousness caused Shelly's heart to skip a beat and for a few seconds, she tried to think of an excuse to get out of sitting in the police station's tiny conference room with the parents of a murdered girl. "I guess I could. I won't be any help."

"We don't know that," Jay said kindly. "We won't know if it's helpful until you do it."

For a quick moment, Shelly wished she had stayed in Boston and had never moved to Paxton Park.

But then, for only a fraction of a second, the image of a field flashed in her mind and was gone.

What was that? What was that?

16

Sitting once again in the cramped, stuffy conference room at the back of the police station, Shelly wished she was any place else. Abby Jackson's mother was slim, well-dressed, had high cheekbones, symmetrical features, and dark brown eyes. Under other circumstances, she would be considered a striking woman, but signs of stress showed in her bloodshot eyes, in the dark, sunken circles under her eyes, and a nervous clasping and unclasping of her hands. It was hard for Shelly to look at the woman ... her misery and distress was so pronounced it was almost tangible.

Mr. Jackson, who wore a white shirt, dark blue jeans, and a navy blazer, sat ram-rod straight in his seat, his face stony and emotionless trying to keep the nightmare of his life in check.

A detective from Springfield had joined the group at Jay's request and he sat at one end of the table. An older man with gray hair and watery blue eyes, he had a calm demeanor and nodded when he was introduced to the parents.

Jay introduced Shelly as an assistant to the department and the Jacksons didn't question her presence in the meeting. Giving a brief summary of where things stood, Jay explained that she wanted to ask some questions and then they could have an open discussion about the state of the investigation.

"Some things I've asked previously, so please bear with me. For the benefit of the others in the room, would you repeat what happened on the morning you realized Abby was not at home?"

Mr. Jackson spoke. "We were up early. We had plans to clean out the shed in the backyard. Abby was due at work and when she didn't get up, Sandra went up to wake her." The man paused and exhaled. "Abby wasn't in her room. The bed hadn't been slept in. We looked in the driveway and her car was missing. We called the police. Sandra called the Walls, the parents of Abby's boyfriend. They told Sandra that Abby wasn't there. They said Abby had dropped Adam off at home around 11pm and he'd been home all night long."

"Had Abby complained about anyone?" Jay asked. "Did she have a fight or a disagreement with anyone? Was there a falling out with a friend?"

"Nothing that we knew of," Mr. Jackson said. "Things seemed normal."

"Did she ever mention anyone flirting with her? Someone being too forward with her?" Jay questioned.

"No, she didn't."

"Had she recently said no to someone who wanted to date her?"

"She hadn't brought anything like that up with us."

"What about her relationship with Adam?" Jay asked. "Were there any bumps in their relationship lately?"

"Not to my knowledge," Mr. Jackson said.

Mrs. Jackson lifted her eyes and nearly whispered. "Abby wasn't sure about continuing her relationship with Adam when they went off to college. She thought they should take a break and see how things went."

"Did she mention if she'd talked to Adam about doing that?"

"She did talk to him. She told me he didn't want to break up or take a break from each other."

Mr. Jackson looked over at his wife. "I didn't know that. You didn't mention that."

"Abby told me about it the day before she disappeared. I just remembered it." The woman used both hands to push her hair back from her face. "I don't know why it slipped my mind. Maybe from the shock of all of this?"

Jay told Mrs. Jackson that things get buried by the mental trauma that accompanies a difficult experience. "It's not unusual at all. That's why we talk multiple times and ask some of the same questions again, in case something, a bit of information or a memory, floats back to the surface. Can you recall if Abby said anything about how Adam took her suggestion to take a break?"

"She told me he got angry."

"What is Adam like? Can you describe him for us?" Jay asked.

Mr. Jackson said, "Adam is a smart young man, athletic. He played on the school football team and did spring track. He's an only child." Jackson winced when he said the words. Abby had been his only daughter. "Adam plans to study pre-med with the intention of going on to medical school."

"Did Adam spend any time at your house?"

"He did," Mr. Jackson said. "He came over for

dinner on occasion or to hang out with Abby. They'd do homework or watch a movie in the family room. He was always pleasant."

"What did you think of Adam, Mrs. Jackson?" Jay asked.

"He was pleasant with us, not overly talkative, but I think that's normal when interacting with your girlfriend's parents."

"He treated Abby well?"

"He did. She always seemed to enjoy his company," Mr. Jackson said and then his brow furrowed. "We heard them arguing one evening. Not a big fight, but they had words. We asked Abby about it, but she brushed it off."

Mrs. Jackson's face seemed to lose some color. "That night. You had gone upstairs to bed after we heard them arguing," she said to her husband and then turned to Jay. "I put some things away in the kitchen and then started up the stairs. I heard Adam say something to Abby. He told her she was *his* girlfriend and no one else's. I didn't like the tone he used, he sounded mean, almost ... menacing." The woman's hand flew to her throat. "Oh. Did Adam...?"

Mr. Jackson reached for her hand. "No ... Adam wouldn't hurt Abby. We've known him for years."

Tears welled in Mrs. Jackson's eyes and she looked from her husband to Jay.

"Were there any other times when you might have heard Adam speak that way to your daughter?" Jay asked.

Mrs. Jackson shook her head. "But he could have talked that way when they were alone."

Shelly's heart thudded hard and the palms of her hands felt clammy. She took a quick glance at the older detective to see him sitting in the same position, his face unreadable.

Jay said, "Abby hurt her back while out running. How did she explain her fall?"

Mr. Jackson said, "Abby said she slipped on some gravel. She was moving fast along the trail, hit the gravel, lost her balance, and fell over the edge of the hill."

"She ran there fairly frequently?" Jay asked.

"She did. It was her regular training run when the team wasn't practicing," Jackson reported.

"She was very familiar with that trail," Jay noted.

"She was." Mr. Jackson nodded.

"Did Adam run on that trail circuit?" Jay asked.

"I suppose he did."

Did Abby and Adam ever run together?"

"Once in a while," Jackson said. "Abby preferred running with her teammates or on her own."

"Did she say why she liked that better?"

Mrs. Jackson piped up. "Abby told me Adam tried to coach her, correct things about her stride, things like that. Abby didn't want him telling her how to run or train. She'd worked all of that out with her coach."

"Adam was only trying to be helpful," Mr. Jackson said.

The more Shelly heard about Adam, the more she would characterize him as being controlling, not helpful.

Jay did not bring up what Shelly had reported to her that a witness claimed to see Adam push Abby on the trail which resulted in her falling into a gulley and injuring her back. That would be discussed after interviewing the witness and speaking again with Adam Wall.

"Abby worked at the resort gift shop this summer," Jay said. "How did she like the job?"

"She didn't like it that much," Mrs. Jackson said. "Abby preferred to be outside and didn't like being cooped up in the store all day. She thought some of the customers could be arrogant and rude. The manager wasn't the best."

"How do you mean about the manager?" Jay asked.

"Abby said he was a pain. Making rude jokes, blaming her for not doing enough if a customer left without making a purchase. Abby said he could be moody, one minute he was sullen, and the next, he was acting childish. She didn't like the man."

"Did the manager ever ask her out?"

A look of shock washed over Mrs. Jackson's face. "I don't think so. Abby never said such a thing. The man was more than twenty years older than Abby."

Shelly didn't think an age difference would stop the manager from making a move on Abby, if he was so inclined.

Jay gave a nod and then brought up Abby's previous work experience. "Abby worked at Glad Hill Farm for a number of years. She enjoyed that job?"

Mrs. Jackson's lips turned up. "Abby loved that farm, she loved everything about being there ... being outside, working with the animals, the people who came to visit the place. She didn't care where she was assigned to work, she loved it all."

"Abby enjoyed the camaraderie there as well," Mr. Jackson said. "Everyone was nice to get along with. They all worked hard, but had fun doing it."

"Dwayne Thomas owns the farm and the orchard. Did Abby have much interaction with him?" Jay questioned.

"Oh, sure," Jackson said. "Dwayne is hands-on. He runs the place, knows everything that is going on. Abby liked working with him."

"Abby thought the world of Dwayne," Mrs. Jackson said. "She said he was a nice man, always concerned about the people who worked there. He pays the employees well. He respects the land, the farm animals." A faraway look showed in the woman's eyes. "I went to the farm right before Abby disappeared and ran into Dwayne. He said how much he missed her not working there this summer. He couldn't believe she'd be off to college in the fall. He looked so sad when he told me he'd probably never see her again. He said he loved Abby." A tear rolled down Mrs. Jackson's cheek and she brushed it away.

What the woman said caused a chill of worry to rush over Shelly. *Dwayne said he loved Abby? That he wouldn't see her again? Did Dwayne...?*

Shelly's heart jumped into her throat.

17

Shelly and Juliet met at the lake after work to kayak and swim and they promised each other there would be no talk of murder and killers for two hours. The day was hot and sunny bringing a lot of people to the water to cool off.

The young women decided to kayak around the perimeter of the lake and by the time they returned to the starting point, their arms had tired from stroking with the paddles.

"Wow, my muscles are sore," Shelly said as she dragged the kayak up on the banking. "I haven't kayaked that far in a very long time."

Perspiration showed on Juliet's arms and forehead. "It was hot out on the water, too. At least we got some good exercise. Now let's jump in and cool off."

Walking up the short hill to the rope swing, they waited in line to zoom out over the water and when it was their turn, each one flew over the lake with a shout and a scream of delight before letting go of the rope and plunging into the cool, crystal, blue water.

Juliet's head broke the surface and she treaded water. "That was great." Her laughter rang in the air.

She and Shelly swam to the edge and bolted up the hill to ride the rope swing again and after, three more plunges, they swam to the raft that was tethered in the middle of the lake to sun themselves. For a while, they shared the raft with a few teenagers who dove and jumped into the water until they all swam for shore to head home.

The sun sank over the tops of the trees and Juliet and Shelly decided to leave the raft and swim back to the beach to towel off and sit on the warm sand. They spread their towels and rested on their backs, eyes closed, soaking up the sun's last rays of the day.

A voice spoke next to them. "Shelly?"

Shelly bolted upright to see the teenaged girl who had spoken to her at Glad Hill Farm about seeing Adam push Abby on the trail causing her to fall down the steep hill. She held her hand to her forehead to shade her eyes. "Dana, hi."

A young man stood next to the slim brunette.

Dana said, "We saw you on the raft. Do you have a few minutes to talk?"

"Sure." Shelly sat cross-legged on her towel and introduced Juliet.

Dana said, "This is William. He's a friend of Abby's boyfriend, Adam."

William nodded to Shelly and Juliet. Worry seemed to tug at his facial muscles making him look older than he was.

Dana said, "I told William that I talked to you about seeing Adam push Abby on the trail. I told him you were nice ... that you gave me good advice. He'd like to talk to you about something that's been bothering him."

"Okay." A wave of anxiety pulsed through Shelly's veins and she was glad to have Juliet sitting beside her. "What's bothering you, William?"

William looked down at his hands. "Adam and I have been friends for a long time. I feel awful talking about him." He let out a long breath. "I heard him talk to Abby. I didn't like the way he was talking to her. He told her she would never be with another man, only him, and if she tried to break off with him, she'd be very sorry."

"When did this happen?" Shelly asked.

"About a month ago. A group of us were hanging

out at the lake one night. Adam was with Abby off to the side of the beach. I overheard the conversation. I didn't like the way it sounded."

"How did Abby react?"

"It was dark so I couldn't see her face very well. She said something to Adam and she started away. Adam grabbed her by the wrist, but Abby yanked away from him." William shook his head. "I walked over to Adam. He was steaming mad. I asked what was wrong."

"What did Adam say?" Juliet asked.

"He ranted about Abby. He said awful things, called her awful names. He said she wasn't grateful, that she was meant for him and him alone. Adam had a few beers. I had never seen him so shook up."

"Had you seen Adam other times when he'd been drinking?" Shelly asked.

"Sure, lots of times, but I'd never heard him say such crazy things before."

"Why do you think he went off on a rant that night?"

"I talked to Abby later, after Adam went home. She told me she wanted to break up with Adam and when she talked to him about how she felt, he went nuts. She said his reaction scared her."

"Do you know what happened after that night?"

Shelly asked. "Adam and Abby were together the night she disappeared so they must have continued to see each other."

"Yeah, they did," William said. "Abby talked to me about it. She still wanted to break up, but decided she wouldn't put an end to the relationship until the day she was going to leave for college. That way she wouldn't have to deal with Adam trying to change her mind and she'd be gone and wouldn't be in the same town with him anymore."

A terrible thought came into Shelly's mind. "Did Abby break up with Adam the night she disappeared?"

"I wondered the same thing," William said. "I don't know if she did or not. Abby was going to leave for college two weeks earlier than she planned. The university had a voluntary outdoor program for incoming freshmen to go hiking and camping in the White Mountains so they could meet some people before school started. Abby loved that kind of stuff and it would get her out of Paxton Park early so she signed up to go."

Shelly asked, "When was she supposed to leave for the trip?"

"About four days after she disappeared." William looked at Dana sitting next to him. "Dana and I have been talking. When she told me she saw Adam push Abby so hard that she fell down the ravine and got injured, well, I thought back to when I heard Adam say those rotten things to Abby. I got worried it wasn't just too much alcohol that made Adam talk to Abby like he owned her. I started to think Adam was losing it, that he was coming unglued."

"What would cause him to unravel?" Shelly asked. "Adam had never shown any indications of becoming unbalanced, had he?"

Sitting in the sand, William leaned forward over his crossed legs. "You know those families where everything looks perfect from the outside? Where everyone is good-looking and smart and seems to have everything going for them? Except they don't."

"You're describing Adam's family?" Juliet eyed the young man.

"Yeah." William dropped his chin. "His parents were nuts. I wouldn't go over there anymore. The place was like a museum. Everything was white. You couldn't drop a crumb. The parents were ridiculously demanding. Adam had to be the best at everything, in school he had to have the best grades, he had to be the best athlete. Did you know Abby was the valedictorian of our class? Adam's mother and father wouldn't let him forget it, that he was only second best and second best was as good as last. The father drank and when he did, he got drunk, and then he'd use Adam and the mother as punching bags, but he was always careful not to hit them where it would show."

William turned his head and looked out over the darkening lake. "I should have spoken up. I should have told our teachers. If I had, maybe Adam wouldn't have...."

"We don't know if Adam has done anything," Shelly reminded the two teenagers.

"He did do something," Dana said as she fiddled nervously with a strand of her long hair. "Adam pushed Abby and she hurt her back. The fall could have been much worse. She could have ended up paralyzed ... the doctor said so."

"As soon as Dana told me what Adam did on that trail, I got real worried," William said. "I haven't told anyone except the three of you what I heard Adam say to Abby. I'm worried he hurt Abby, I'm worried he might have killed her."

Even in the dying light, Shelly could see William's face take on a look like he felt ill from accusing his old friend. "It's good you're talking about this. I know you don't want Adam to get into trouble, but it's worse to protect someone who might be dangerous. Have the police talked to you?"

"Yes." William hung his head.

"You didn't tell them what you've just told us?" Shelly asked.

"No." The word slipped softly from William's throat. "I should have. I just couldn't. It didn't seem right. Adam had too much to drink that night and I was sure that what he said to Abby was fueled by the beer. I thought it would all be back to normal the next day. Then Abby told me she wanted to get away from Adam, that he scared her. And then Dana and I got to talking. I was torn about telling the police. I wished they'd come back and talk to me because I didn't want to go there and show up out of the blue. What if I'm wrong and I get the police thinking the wrong way about Adam?" William rubbed hard at his forehead and Dana put her arm around his shoulders.

Dana said, "The police were nice when I went to talk to them. They listened to me and they said I could speak anonymously. They'll do the same for you." She looked to Shelly and Juliet. "You think William should tell the police what he just told you?"

The young women spoke almost in unison. "Yes."

The teenagers thanked Shelly and Juliet for their help and left the beach to go to the parking area.

"Why do you think they told us all of that? Why didn't they talk to their parents or some friends?" Juliet asked.

Shelly watched Dana and William walk away. "Sometimes, it's easier to talk to someone who isn't connected to your circle in order to get a different perspective or opinion on what's going on."

"It sure seems like Adam is a strong suspect," Juliet said.

"Yeah." Shelly nodded, even though she had the nagging feeling there was something missing from the puzzle. But what was it?

18

After work, Shelly and Jack set out to hike up to the summit lodge of the mountain. Jack asked if it was too soon for Shelly to expect to make the hike to the top, but she told him she was feeling much better, her ribs had healed and she was able to take deep breaths. Even though her leg would tire, she told Jack, if they could take it slow, she wanted to give it a try. "There are delicious pastries and coffees at the lodge so that will be my incentive to make it to the top," she explained with a smile.

The two hikers paused every now and then so Shelly could sit and rest her leg and they found a spot off the trail with a rocky ledge where they could stand and look out over the tree tops to a magnificent view of the land stretching out below. Emerald green fields, meandering streams, sparkling lakes, and the distant mountains looked glorious under the late afternoon sun.

"It's amazing, isn't it?" Shelly couldn't tear her eyes away from the natural beauty before her.

"No matter the season, seeing these views always makes me feel calm and peaceful," Jack told her.

They stood quietly staring out at the spectacular sight until Shelly broke the silence. "I've never driven on the road that goes up to the summit." She turned and looked at Jack.

"The road winds around the mountain up to the top. Whoever designed its location did a great job. There are spots to stop along the way to park and take in the views, but for the most part, the road doesn't interfere with the trails and the peace and quiet of hiking or biking to the summit."

"You've driven the road?" Shelly's face was serious.

"Yeah." Jack nodded. "Why do you ask?"

Taking in a deep breath, she let her eyes wander over the expansive scene. "Are there any spots off the road, like cliffs? Are there any spots where a car could go off the road and plummet down?"

Jack gave the question some thought. "No. There

are boulders and heavy guardrails wherever the road gets close to the edge. Maybe a truck could plow through them, but certainly not a car. Why?"

Shelly couldn't tell him she'd dreamt of Abby's car floating in the air and then crashing down into the earth. "I wondered if Abby's killer might have pushed her car, with her in it, off a cliff around here. If it was a certain kind of spot, it might be hard to see a car that had driven off the road."

The idea of such a thing caused Jack's mouth to turn down. "I don't think it would be possible. If someone did manage to get the car off the road and through the boulders or the guardrails, there would be visible damage at the point where the car crashed through. Someone would definitely notice that."

"There are fire roads through the woods," Shelly said. "Do any of them come close to the edge? Could a vehicle crash down part of the mountain by going off one of the fire roads?"

"The fire roads are more interior lanes. They don't go near the edge. There aren't any steep drop-offs where the fire roads are located except for maybe a gulley or shorter, steep decline, something like that. I think a hiker might notice if a car had gone off the side of one of the fire roads."

"There are so many of those lanes though. It

might take a while for someone to find a car that went off one of the most remote roads," Shelly said.

"That's true."

"What about one of the lakes?" Shelly asked. "Someone could push the car into a lake. It would sink to the bottom. No one would see it."

"The police have had helicopters fly over the lakes with spotters onboard looking for anything amiss," Jack said. "They've had divers investigating, too."

"I didn't know that."

"Some of the lakes are pretty deep," Jack said. "I guess a car could be missed, but I know the police divers have found several submerged vehicles in these lakes."

"Maybe Abby's SUV isn't in one of these lakes then." Shelly's voice sounded sad.

Jack's shoulders drooped. "I hope the police can figure this crime out soon. Not only for Abby and her parents' sakes, but for the town's sake as well. The manager of the adventure tours told us that people are cancelling reservations like crazy. The fall is a huge tourist season with people coming to the mountain to view the foliage, hike, bike, canoe. Management is in a panic right now. If the tourists don't come, there are going to be layoffs. It will hurt the town's economy, the restaurants and shops will be hurting. It's a real mess."

Shelly's face clouded. "I haven't given that much thought lately. I didn't realize how Abby's murder could impact almost everyone in town."

"We'll keep our fingers crossed that the killer will be caught soon, for everyone's safety and for the town's businesses." Jack gestured back to the trail. "Should we head home or do you want to continue up?"

Shelly gave Jack a grin. "Let's keep going. I want one of those pastries."

Another hour passed and Shelly and Jack emerged from the trail onto the summit where steel ramps led to a high viewing platform and the log cabin café and restaurant stood under a cluster of small pines.

"We made it." Shelly said with excitement.

"How's your leg?" Jack asked.

"I won't be able to walk for a week and you might need to carry me back down," Shelly kidded, "but it was definitely worth it."

Jack let out a hearty laugh. "I'd be happy to carry you down."

They climbed up to the viewing platform and admired the beautiful panoramic views before heading to the café for their tasty reward. Shelly ordered coffee and a slice of cheesecake and Jack had iced tea and a hot fudge sundae which they carried to a table near the windows and joined a few people they knew from working at the resort.

Chatter moved from one topic to another before centering on Abby Jackson's murder and its ramifications.

"The police need to catch this guy. People are on edge, they're afraid the killer will strike again," one young man said.

"Tourists are going elsewhere," another person in the group said. "We can't afford to lose the tourists. It will cause a lot of financial problems for most people in town."

"There's an undercurrent of panic in town," a woman told them. "Worry, fear, a feeling the police aren't doing enough."

Shelly didn't mention that Jay was barely getting a few hours of sleep a night and was consumed with every aspect and detail of the case.

Tony, a friend of Jack's, sat across the table from Shelly and her boyfriend. "It's like a bunch of dominoes going down, one thing leads to another. My sister works in the office at Glad Hill Farm. She told me Dwayne Thomas has been knocked to his knees by Abby's murder and from finding the hand. He's on meds for anxiety, he's become mentally dull, is making lots of mistakes. If that farm loses business, it will be a disaster. The place employs tons of people from the area."

Shelly asked, "What kind of mistakes is Dwayne making?"

Tony said, "My sister told me that Dwayne moved money from the farm bank account into his personal account and there wasn't enough money to pay the supply vendors. It took a while to sort out and some of the vendors are mighty angry and had to be cajoled into not taking their business elsewhere. Dwayne started a project on the west side of his property. He wants to add a winery to the farm. The cost is way too high and Paul Blake, the nephew, thinks it's a terrible, risky financial move so he halted the building plans. My sister said it's been lucky that Paul has been around to set things right."

Tony shook his head. "That's only one example of how this murder is impacting people and can cause a chain reaction of trouble throughout the town."

Jeff brought up the possible layoffs that might be

coming to the resort if guests continue to cancel their reservations and while the two men discussed the issue, Shelly's thoughts strayed to Dwayne and his instability and began to wonder if his mental decline had started *before* Abby's disappearance. What Abby's mother's told them in the interview the other day rang in her head. Dwayne loved Abby. He was afraid he'd never see her again after she left for college.

Cold sweat beaded up on her back. Was Dwayne in the first stages of dementia? Did he become obsessed with Abby? Was her upcoming departure to college upsetting Dwayne so much that he wanted to prevent it? Did Dwayne...?

Shelly's worries were interrupted by Jack's voice. "Shelly?"

She shook herself back to the present and forced a smile. "Sorry. I was lost in my own thoughts. What did you ask?"

"How is business at the diner?" Jack asked. "Have you noticed a drop off in people coming in?"

"Um. I'm not sure," Shelly said. "There hasn't been a decrease yet in orders for baked goods for either the diner or the resort bakery. Hopefully, the crime will be solved soon and things can go back to normal for the town businesses."

Thoughts about Dwayne Thomas's mental state swirled in Shelly's mind and made her heart pound. She needed to talk to Jay.

Has Dwayne lost touch with reality? *Did Dwayne kill Abby?*

19

S helly arrived early for her baking job at Glad Hill Farm and was asked by the main chef if she'd mind waiting thirty minutes to begin since they were still using the counter where she did her work. The day was less hot than it had been and the air was clear and comfortable so Shelly decided to take a walk around the farm to pass the time.

Approaching a small lake not far from the food barn, she spotted a figure sitting on a bench facing the water. She walked over and greeted the man. "Hi, Dwayne. What a beautiful day. May I join you?"

Dwayne glanced up at Shelly and shielded his eyes from the sun. At first, the expression on his face showed confusion as if he had no idea who the woman was who was speaking to him, but then his eyes brightened. "Shelly. Have a seat."

When she sat down next to Dwayne, he said, "I've always liked sitting here looking at the water at the end of a day's work."

"It's a lovely spot," Shelly agreed. "Are you finished working for the day?"

Dwayne checked his watch. "Oh, I guess not. It's earlier than I thought." The man had dark circles under his eyes and he gave the impression that he was sleepy or lacking in energy.

"Are you okay?" Shelly asked.

"Me? Sure." Dwayne seemed to wonder why she would ask such a question.

"Can you tell me what Abby Jackson was like?" Shelly wanted to see what the older man would say.

"Abby?" Dwayne's expression softened and a slight smile crossed his lips. "She was an angel. She reminded me of my late wife. If we'd had a daughter, she would have been like Abby. Abby loved this farm, the outdoors, everything about it. We got along great. It made me happy to be around her."

"She was a good worker?"

"The best." Dwayne nodded a few times.

"She was planning to head to college this fall," Shelly said.

"Yes. She was a smart young woman." Dwayne rubbed at one of his wrists. "I was going to miss her. I loved that girl."

"You found her hand?" Shelly hated to bring it up, but she needed to see Dwayne's reaction.

The man seemed to shrink into himself. "Yes."

"Where did you find it?"

Dwayne adjusted his position and looked into Shelly's eyes. "In the orchard. Abby loved the orchard." He closed his eyes for a few seconds and didn't open them until Shelly spoke.

"Are you sure you're feeling okay?"

Dwayne's eyelids flicked open. "I'm okay, just tired is all."

"Maybe you should go home and have a nap?" Shelly suggested.

"What's the point? I'll still be tired when I wake up." Dwayne looked out over the water again. "Nothing will have changed," he whispered. The man turned to Shelly again. "Are you alone?"

Shelly blinked, not understanding the question. "How do you mean?"

"Do you feel alone in the world?"

Shelly's breath caught in her throat for a moment ... sometimes that was exactly how she felt. "I've made a good friend since I moved here and

I've met some nice people. I have a new boyfriend, too."

"I'm glad for you." Dwayne patted her hand. "I'm alone in the world."

Shelly's heart clenched at his words. "But you have your sister and your nephew, Paul, and all the people who work here with you."

Dwayne shook his head. "I'm alone," he said softly. "Abby knew what I meant." Drawing a long breath into his lungs, he asked, "Do you want me to show you where I found her hand?"

Shelly opened her mouth, but didn't know what to say.

A man called out to them and Shelly looked back to see Paul striding across the grass towards them. "Hello, you two. Soaking up the sun?"

Shelly explained that the kitchen area she used wasn't available yet. "I've been talking with Dwayne." She stood up and made eye contact with Paul and when she spoke, she used a quiet voice. "Dwayne seems like he might be under the weather or maybe coming down with something."

Paul walked around to take a look at his uncle. "Why don't you go in and have some tea with Betsey? She was asking me where you were. She put the kettle on already."

"Sounds like a good idea." Dwayne stood and started away, but stopped and turned his attention to Shelly. "You're smart, too. I can tell."

When Dwayne had tottered away to the office building, Paul asked, "What was he going on about?"

Shelly didn't know why, but she didn't want to tell Paul the details of her interaction. "We were talking about the farm. I was concerned about him. He seemed sapped of energy. He wasn't like that when I've spoken with him before."

"His mental decline seems to be accelerating." Paul watched Dwayne open the office's door and go inside. "I've been wondering if Dwayne has been experiencing dementia and then when he found that young girl's hand, the whole thing sent him into a downward spiral. I'm taking him to see the doctor next week."

"That seems like a good idea." Shelly looked over her shoulder.

"He might need to be hospitalized for a little while to do some tests on him." Paul rubbed the back of his neck. "See if they can get to the bottom of what's wrong with him."

"Have you ever seen him angry?" Shelly asked.

"Occasionally. Not long ago, he threw his shoes across the room at me."

"Why did he do that? What upset him?" Shelly asked.

Paul said, "He was muttering and cursing under his breath. I couldn't make out why he got angry at me."

"You're living in the house with him?"

Paul gave a nod. "He shouldn't be alone. I have the cabin not far from here that Dwayne had built for me years ago so I'd have a place to stay when I came to work on marketing plans for the farm. I haven't been using it. I want to be near my uncle in case he needs anything."

"Have you given up your other clients?" Shelly asked.

"No, I haven't. I'm able to work remotely for them." Paul let out a sigh. "It's a lucky thing I'm able to stay here until we figure out what to do with Dwayne."

"How is your mother taking it?"

"She's very upset about it," Paul said. "My mother doesn't understand what could be wrong with Dwayne. She doesn't want to face the fact that Uncle Dwayne might have to move into a facility where they're able to handle dementia."

"It seems odd that your uncle would go downhill so quickly," Shelly thought out loud.

When Paul shot her a look, Shelly thought she saw a flash of anger pass over his face.

"Why odd? It happens." Paul's mouth tightened.

"I only meant it seemed very fast," Shelly said. "Just a little more than a week ago, I had several very pleasant conversations with Dwayne. He seemed fine. Today, he almost seems like a different person. Maybe his medication should be checked to be sure he isn't taking too much or that what the doctors put him on is what he needs."

There was a sharpness to Paul's tone when he told Shelly, "Like I said, in some cases, it isn't unusual for decline to happen quickly." He shoved a hand into the back pocket of his jeans.

Shelly realized she'd offended Paul by asking personal questions about Dwayne's situation. "I'm sure the doctors will figure it out and provide Dwayne with what he needs."

Paul looked towards the office. "I'd better get back to work. Nice talking to you."

Shelly headed back to the kitchen, her mind working over the interactions with Dwayne and Paul. It was clear from what Dwayne said about Abby that he adored her. Was he so upset that Abby was moving away that he did something to be sure she would never leave him? Why did he ask if Shelly felt alone? Why does Dwayne feel so alone? Is his illness confusing his emotions?

"Shelly." A young woman's voice called to her.

Shelly saw Dana, the teenager who worked at the farm coming towards her.

"Are you working today?" Dana asked.

"I am."

Dana said, "William went to the police station today to tell them what he heard Adam say to Abby. After talking with you and Juliet, he felt he had an obligation to report his worries that Adam might have hurt Abby."

"He did the right thing," Shelly said.

"I was working in the petting zoo," Dana said. "I'm going to work the food barn counter now. I saw you sitting with Dwayne by the lake. How was he?"

"He seemed tired," Shelly said.

"I'm worried about him. Do you think he has dementia?"

"I don't know. I guess it's possible. The family will get him the help he needs."

Dana scoffed. "Will they?"

"Why do you say that?" Shelly asked.

"Have you met the other owner? Dwayne's sister? Nora Blake?"

"She lives down the street from me," Shelly said. "I met her briefly."

"Old Nora hates the farm." Dana kicked a pebble as she walked along the path with Shelly. "She gives me the impression that she's selfish and self-interested. All she cares about is spending money, going on trips, buying things. I bet she hopes Dwayne dies so she can sell the place."

"Sell it? Wouldn't she keep it running? The farm must bring in a good amount of money."

"She'd sell it," Dana said. "It's too much trouble, it's too much work. Most everyone here thinks Nora's motto is *take the money and run*."

"What about Paul? He could run it for his mother."

"Yuck, I hope not," Dana said. "Paul's a creep. He's always leering at us. You should have seen him with Abby. She couldn't stand him."

They turned up the walk to the food barn passing visitors going in and coming out. Before Shelly could ask anything about Paul, Dana said goodbye. "I better hurry. I'm late and I need to change." She started for the employee entrance. "Thanks for talking with William. You've been a big help to us."

Shelly pressed a finger to her temple. A doozy of a headache was coming on. *What's going on around here?*

20

"I thought the best place would be along the back fence since that section of the yard is sunny most of the day." Shelly pointed to the ground in front of the fence.

Juliet leaned on the handle of a shovel looking wary about the amount of work that had to be done. "Wait a minute. How big is this thing going to be?"

Shelly walked in a rectangular pattern starting and ending at different sections of the fence. "Like this."

"Okay, good. I worried you were putting in the garden along the entire fence."

Shelly smiled. "Even if that was the plan, this yard isn't exactly big. The garden I'm planning will give both us plenty of vegetables next year." Shelly wanted to dig out a garden plot and add fertile soil to it so most of the heavy work would be done. In the spring, she would clean up the garden, add nutrients to the soil, turn it over, and plant the vegetables.

Justice trilled from her supervising spot on the patio lounge chair.

Shelly nodded to the cat. "See, Justice agrees with the plan."

"Okay, tell me what to do." Juliet stepped forward with her shovel at the ready.

After two hours of removing the grass, struggling to dig out big rocks, and turning over the soil, the two friends, dripping sweat, collapsed into chairs on the patio.

"I have a new appreciation for farming and working the land." Juliet had a smudge of soil on her cheek.

"Is this your first garden?" Shelly asked.

"Yes, and my last." Juliet leaned her head back on the cushion and closed her eyes. "Too bad you're not putting in a swimming pool instead."

"I don't think the landlord would approve," Shelly said. "He was slightly reluctant about okaying the garden. He finally agreed to it when I told him if I didn't renew the lease, I'd take out the garden and return the backyard to the way it was."

"Clever." Juliet still hadn't opened her eyes. "May

I have an ice cold drink, please, before I need to be hospitalized from all that hard labor?"

Chuckling, Shelly went inside and returned with a little cat treat for Justice and two tall glasses of lemonade with ice cubes clinking against the sides.

"Heavenly," Juliet sighed after the first sip and held the glass against the side of her face. "I can go on living."

Shelly adjusted the patio umbrella for maximum shade and she, Juliet, and the cat rested in the chairs with a light breeze rustling the leaves on the trees.

"You had some interesting conversations at the farm yesterday," Juliet noted. "What do you think is going on with Dwayne?"

"I really don't know what to think." Shelly sighed. "It could be dementia or maybe, his behavior is due to the trauma and upset of Abby's murder and finding her hand in the orchard. He lost his wife and son years ago, then a young woman he was very fond of ends up murdered. He's on medication ... maybe it's not the correct prescription or it could be the wrong dosage."

"Or maybe it's a combination of those things," Juliet offered. "He may have the beginnings of dementia which became amplified by the murder and by the medication he's taking now."

"Good points." Shelly took a sip from her drink.

"Do you think Dwayne is a suspect?"

"I think he has to be," Shelly said. "The things he said about never seeing Abby again if she left for college and that he loved her. Could his behavior be a mental reaction to having killed Abby? He might have killed her in a moment of anger or rage and now regrets what he's done."

"That's a definite possibility." Juliet nodded, thinking it over.

"I don't know. He seems like a nice man. He has a very kind energy."

Juliet said, "If Dwayne is in mental decline though, his personality could change. He might have killed Abby in a moment when he lost touch with reality, and now recalls what he did, and is suffering remorse over it."

"No wonder Dwayne told me he feels alone," Shelly said. "His sister, Nora, doesn't care about the farm and would sell it and his nephew, Paul, is taking more control of the business. Dwayne seemed so exhausted yesterday, almost out of it. When I interviewed for the baking job, he was energetic and conversational. How quickly he's fallen into this stupor."

Justice had lifted her head and seemed to be listening to the humans' speculations.

"And what about Adam Wall, Abby's boyfriend?" Juliet asked. "He is definitely one to name as a suspect."

Shelly said, "That's for sure. Right now, I'd put my money on Adam being the killer. I bet he left his parents' house after Abby dropped him off, went to find her, confronted her, ended up fighting, and now she's dead."

"After hearing how he pushed Abby on the trail and she fell down the hill, I thought he was the murderer. It seems he has a lot of bottled up rage inside of him. You said he seemed almost arrogant when you sat in with Jay when she interviewed him."

"He had an attitude," Shelly said. "He showed no visible emotion over losing Abby. Adam definitely had an edge to him. There were moments when I was unsure if I believed what he was saying."

"It sounds like he had a difficult home life. Everything had to be perfect. He was pressured by his parents to be the best and if he wasn't, they berated him mercilessly. Poor kid. What kind of life is that? Unending striving for perfection." Juliet groaned.

"Adam must have seen it as a failure when Abby wanted to break off their relationship," Shelly pointed out. "Maybe failing at something was the biggest issue."

"And don't forget, Abby was the senior class valedictorian," Juliet said. "Abby beat Adam academically and then didn't want to be with him anymore. Those were two blows to Adam's ego."

"I could see him wanting to strike out at Abby," Shelly said. "The police will never be able to prove Adam left his house that night and met up with Abby again. I wonder if he texted her to come back."

"The police would have the records of any texts and calls Adam sent or made, so he couldn't have contacted Abby with his phone," Juliet said.

"That's true." Shelly's eyes brightened. "They don't live far apart ... one or two blocks from each other. Adam could have jogged over to Abby's house, cutting through the neighbors' yards. He might have arrived just before she got home or right as she was pulling into the driveway. Maybe he asked her to drive around, then they got into a fight, and he killed her."

"But don't cell phones give off signals?" Juliet asked. "Cell towers know which phones are nearby. There are records of that. If Abby and Adam were driving around together after he said she'd dropped him at home, there would be records of where they went by searching the tower's phone records."

"Are the records that detailed?" Shelly asked. "Do they pinpoint the exact time and place a phone has been or is it more broad than that?"

Juliet shrugged. "I don't know, but the police must have looked into all of this."

"Is Abby's phone missing?" Shelly asked.

"I don't know that either."

"Adam could have left his phone at home before he went to Abby's house," Shelly suggested.

"How likely is that? A young man leaving his phone at home?" Juliet's eyebrow raised. "Unless the murder was premeditated. If Adam planned to do Abby harm, he might have left his phone in his bedroom."

"If only someone saw Adam out after he claimed he was at home," Shelly said.

"I'm sure the police would like that kind of information, too." Juliet smiled and Shelly reached over and gave her friend's arm a bop.

"The police have obviously looked into all of these things." Shelly shook her head. "And here, I thought I was a criminal investigating genius because I came up with all of these ideas."

"I guess you should stick to baking." Juliet kidded as she took a swallow of her lemonade.

"You're right, I should," Shelly said. "Is there anyone else who is on the suspect radar?"

Juliet looked over at her friend. "I thought you were going to stick to baking and leave this to the police."

"Jay asked me to help," Shelly defended herself.

"Yes, with dreams." A serious expression pulled at Juliet's facial muscles and she asked with a suspicious tone, "Any new dreams lately?"

"I've had dreams, but none relating to what's going on."

"Has Lauren been in the dreams?" Juliet pushed herself up straighter on the lounge chair.

"No, she hasn't." Sadness permeated Shelly's voice.

"Are you pushing too hard?" Juliet asked softly.

"What do you mean?"

Juliet asked, "Are you wound up about dreaming when you go to bed? Are you anxious that you won't have a useful dream? Are you worried you'll have a disturbing dream?"

"Yes, to all of those things." Shelly rubbed at the tension in her shoulders.

"Maybe you need to take the pressure off," Juliet

said. "Have some warm milk before bed, take a nice bath, play some soothing music, let your mind relax. Don't keep going over and over things. Your brain needs quiet time to put things together, to make connections."

Justice sat up and trilled her approval.

"The cat agrees with me," Juliet smiled.

"Two teaming up together to set me straight?" Shelly chuckled. "Okay, then. Your suggestions sound really good. I have to admit I'm feeling mentally weary. I'll take your advice, starting tonight."

21

The farm bustled with activity as the tourists and locals made purchases in the gift shop, took their children into the petting zoo, walked around the lake, visited the brewery, picked out fruits and vegetables from the veggie stand and bought jars of honey made by the farm's bees. The cooler weather made people think of fall and drew them out to the farm.

Looking at everyone enjoying the place, Shelly thought if the farm was any indication, it sure didn't look like the town was headed for any economic trouble.

Arriving early for her baking job, she hoped to run into Dwayne so she could have a talk with him, but as Shelly walked around, she didn't spot him anywhere causing a wave of unease to run through her, worrying that the man might have taken a turn for the worse.

A woman trying to get around a family of five who were strolling on the walkway, bumped into Shelly and when she turned to apologize, she recognized the farm's new baker. "Oh, hi," the woman gave a warm smile. "I met you on the first day. I'm Angela. I do the payroll."

The women chatted for a few minutes and then Shelly asked, "Have you seen Dwayne? I was looking for him."

"I haven't seen him today." Angela pointed to the lake. "He's been walking a lot lately. He's been going around the lake and on the trails that lead out past the orchard."

Shelly checked her watch for the time. "I have an hour before I start baking. Maybe I'll see if I can run into him." She thanked the woman and headed for the trails knowing that a lot of people would be out walking on them.

Almost ready to give up and head back to the farm's kitchen, Shelly noticed a lone figure standing on a bluff near the orchard and she hiked up the trail to find Dwayne looking out over the farmland.

When he saw her, a smile spread over his face. "It's my talented baker."

"How are you feeling?" Shelly asked the man.

"I have some energy today. I must have had a bad cold or a flu ... it seems to have knocked me out."

"I'm glad you're better."

"See the view from here? Over that way is the food barn and the petting zoo and the gift shop. See how pretty the lake looks? This way is the orchard and over there is the spot for the fall corn maze." Dwayne pointed.

Shelly realized Dwayne must have forgotten he had already shown her the farm from this vantage point. She asked, "How many acres do you own?"

"Over five-hundred. There used to be more, but we sold some acreage to the resort."

"You've done a remarkable job running the place. It's a very popular destination."

"It had to be done," Dwayne said. "It's difficult these days making a family farm profitable. That's why we added all of these attractions."

"People love it," Shelly told him.

"I had an idea to start a winery, grow the grapes, make the wines, have a tasting room for people to come and enjoy the wines." Dwayne's eyes darkened.

"I bet that would be really popular. There isn't a winery for miles around here. The resort visitors would love that." When she noticed Dwayne's expression she asked him what was wrong.

"Paul put a stop to the winery plans." The older man shoved his hands into his back pockets. "Don't ever get old, young lady. It gives people a reason to dismiss your ideas and plans. They don't take you serious, your ideas are old-fashioned, you're not able to think things through, you don't understand modern demands. That's what I hear all the time."

"Paul says those things to you?"

"Paul thinks he's a hot shot marketer. He wants to branch out into project development. The man does a good job, but his ideas are the only ones that matter."

"What does Paul think you should do with the land the winery would go on?" Shelly asked.

"Paul wants the Christmas tree farm. He's started the work on it." Dwayne made a harrumphing sound. "He says it will draw people to the farm in the winter when things are slow. I like the idea, but not at the expense of the winery."

"Can you two work it out?" Shelly asked.

"Paul forgets that I'm the owner here. He thinks

he can toss out my plans, but he's wrong." Dwayne's face was turning red with anger. "Paul tells people I'm losing my mind. I heard him. The man is over-stepping his bounds."

Shelly worried that Dwayne was getting too wound up.

He ranted against Paul for a few more minutes, and then said, "I'm very tired." Dwayne's eyes took on a faraway look and he reached for Shelly's arm. "Would you walk me back down to the farm?" His voice was feeble and his shoulders drooped. His face took on that spaced-out look that Shelly had seen the other day. Whatever boost in energy and mental clarity the man had experienced, it had now disappeared.

Shelly held to Dwayne's arm and they descended the bluff, walked back along the trails, and at last, returned to the main part of the farm where the visitors were moving from attraction to attraction.

"I'd like to sit by the lake," Dwayne told Shelly.

"Are you sure you don't want to go back to your house?" she asked

"I want to sit."

Shelly deposited the older man at an empty bench facing the water.

"You're very kind," Dwayne patted her hand.

Explaining she had to go make the pies, she started away.

"Don't be alone, Shelly," Dwayne told her. "And don't grow old either. I don't recommend it."

Smiling at the man, Shelly told him, "I'll do my best."

RETURNING HOME FROM THE FARM, Shelly rode her bicycle down her street and spotted Jay's police cruiser parked in Juliet's driveway. Jay and Juliet looked up when they saw Shelly approaching, and waved her over. From the looks on their faces, they were discussing something serious.

Shelly stopped her bike and still straddling it, looked from Jay to Juliet. "What's going on? Has there been a break in the case?"

"Not really a break," Jay said. "I'd call it more of an interesting development."

"What happened?" Shelly couldn't wait to hear the news.

"It turns out Adam Wall was not inside his parents' house from 11pm on." Jay slipped her thumb into her belt.

"Where was he? Did someone report seeing him?" Shelly asked with excitement tinging her words.

"Mr. Wall came to the station yesterday. He said he woke up around 1am to use the bathroom and he noticed light under his son's bedroom door. He opened it a crack to see if Adam was still up or had fallen asleep. Adam wasn't there."

"Does the father know where Adam went?" Shelly asked.

Jay said, "He reported that Adam told him he had gone out with his friend, William. William denies this."

"William?" Shelly's eyes were wide. "He was the one who told me he heard Adam say a lot of bad things to Abby."

"Right. He came to talk to us at the station," Jay said. "He told us he didn't go anywhere with Adam that night."

"So Adam's lying," Juliet said.

"So it seems." Jay's lips were thin and tight and her eyelids drooped from the effects of fatigue. "It is also concerning that the father has gone all this time without telling us he knew Adam was not at home during the night."

"Where does Adam say he went?" Shelly asked.

Jay said, "He says he went to the mountain with William, had a couple of beers he took from his family's refrigerator, and then went home."

"But William says he wasn't with Adam." Juliet leaned against the police cruiser.

"It may have been the story Adam made up to tell his mother and father," Jay said. "He's coming into the station with his parents in an hour for another discussion with us. We'll see what he says this time. And we have to be very attentive to what the parents say since they've shown us they aren't bothered by lying to us."

"It's the case of presenting perfection to the world," Shelly said. "Everything is wonderful in their house, nothing ever goes wrong. They'll even lie to the police to preserve their façade."

"The important question is," Juliet said, "where was Adam that night?"

"Has anyone reported seeing Adam during the night?" Shelly asked.

"We're talking to some people," Jay said.

Juliet caught Shelly's eye and winked. "That's Jay-lingo for *I can't tell you anything.*"

"This might be important information that will crack the case," Shelly said.

"Don't get too hopeful yet," Jay said. "We've a long way to go. Just because this guy lied to his parents, and to us, about sneaking out of the house at night, it doesn't make him a killer. It's a huge jump to go from sneaking out at night to committing murder." Jay checked the time. "I'd better get back to the station."

Juliet said, "Shelly has heard some interesting things regarding Dwayne Thomas over at Glad Hill Farm."

Jay looked at Shelly. "Can it wait until we talk again?"

"Oh, sure." Shelly gave a nod. "Good luck with the Wall family today."

Jay got into the cruiser and drove away down the street.

"So that little good-for-nothing bully might actually be Abby's killer." Juliet's tone was full of anger and disgust. "They should arrest him and end this mess."

"What about due process?" Shelly asked her friend. "What if he's innocent? He might be an unlikable, arrogant, egotistical jerk, but that isn't reason to slap him with a murder charge."

"Oh, I know," Juliet groaned. "I'm just tired of people like the ones in this family. Their actions and inactions cause a lot of hurt and trouble and misery. Why can't people be good to each other?"

Shelly put her arm around her friend's shoulders.

Yes. Why can't they?

22

_____

While Shelly picked a few weeds from the front bed and filled the watering can to give the flowers a drink, Justice sat on the bottom step of the cottage's porch watching the young woman work. It was early evening and as the sun headed for the horizon, streaks of rose and lavender painted the sky.

When she finished with the flower bed, Shelly looked at the cat. "Want to stroll around the neighborhood?"

Justice rose from her seat on the steps, arched her back in a huge stretch, and then padded down to the sidewalk and led the way along the lane with Shelly walking a couple of steps behind the furry, Calico feline.

Shelly had only met and talked with several

people who lived on the street, but she recognized many others from her evening walks around the neighborhood who were out working in their yards and giving her a wave as she and the cat passed by.

As they approached Nora Blake's home, the older woman drove up and pulled into her driveway. When she stepped out, she noticed Shelly and called a greeting to her.

"Out with that cat-dog of yours?" Nora stood staring at Justice. "I have never seen a cat go for a walk with someone before."

Shelly smiled down at the sweet animal. "Justice is one-of-a-kind."

Nora removed a suitcase from the backseat.

"Where you away?" Shelly asked.

"Just for a few days." Nora set down the suitcase and walked over to chat with Shelly. "Sometimes I think I should sell my house. I'm away from home more than I'm here. A friend called and invited me to New York City for a visit. I've been thinking of selling and just renting a small apartment for when I'm actually around here."

"That might be a good idea if you aren't at home very often," Shelly agreed.

"I could put the money into investments and make a nice return on it." Nora looked at her house. "I've been here a long time and it would be hard to leave, but I can take my memories with me."

"Have you seen your brother recently?" Shelly asked.

"I haven't. I left for New York shortly after I got back from Europe. I barely had time to do some laundry before I was off again."

"Have you talked to him?"

Nora turned to look closely at Shelly. "I haven't. Are you working at the farm? Did Dwayne hire you for the baking?"

"He did, yes. He's...."

Nora narrowed her eyes. "He's what?"

"Have you talked to Paul?" Shelly asked.

Nora placed a hand on her hip and creases formed between her eye brows. "I've been traveling. I haven't talked to anyone. Why do you keep asking? Is something wrong?"

"Dwayne seems ... different."

"Different, how? Stop beating around the bush and tell me what's going on."

"Dwayne was on medication for anxiety after finding Abby Jackson's hand." Shelly paused.

"I know that."

"Your brother has become forgetful, sort of ...

spaced out. He's not himself. Paul told me that Dwayne has a doctor's appointment next week."

Nora's face looked pinched. "It would have been nice if Paul contacted me about this," she muttered. "Have you talked to Dwayne?"

"A few times." Shelly gave a nod.

"What's he like?"

Shelly said, "He's quiet, lacks energy, seems fatigued, he shows little emotion, he has a flat affect."

Justice hissed.

"He isn't working?" Nora looked concerned.

"He was, but recently he isn't doing a lot. I only see him once in a while. You should talk to Paul." Shelly didn't want to get in the middle of the family's troubles.

"Maybe Paul can handle it." Nora put her hand on the side of her face. "I'm sure he can. I'm supposed to leave tomorrow for Palm Springs. I'm considering moving there with a friend. We've had the trip planned for a month." The woman looked at Shelly. "Don't breathe a word of my possible move. Don't tell a soul. No one knows about it. I'll make the final decision once I'm out there again. I've had enough of the winter. I want to live somewhere warm." She nodded. "I'll give Paul a call to find out what's going on with Dwayne."

"That's a good idea," Shelly said.

Nora took a step closer to the young woman. "What has Paul said to you? Have you talked to Paul?"

"We've talked a little. He just expressed some concern over Dwayne's health issues." Shelly was intentionally vague.

Nora groaned. "Why did this have to happen now when I'm so busy."

Shelly's eyes widened in surprise at Nora's self-interest.

"I'd better get going." Shelly and Justice started away. "Good luck with your trip. I hope Dwayne is feeling better soon."

Walking around the block with the cat, Shelly thought over the conversation with Nora and wondered about her and Dwayne's relationship. Why hadn't Paul called her to talk about Dwayne's problems? Maybe the family isn't close. Dwayne had told her that he felt alone.

Didn't Paul tell me his mother was upset over Dwayne's health? Then why did Nora act like she didn't know what was going on with Dwayne?

It was nearly dark when Shelly and Justice climbed the steps and went inside the cottage. With a grumbling stomach, Shelly fed the cat and then made an omelette, tossed a salad, and warmed a roll in the oven. Carrying her plate to the living room sofa, she lit a candle, put on some music, and sat down to enjoy her dinner with Justice curled next to her.

After finishing her meal, Shelly got a pen and a pad of paper and started making notes on the suspects, facts, and details of Abby's disappearance and probable murder. She stood and began pacing back and forth across the room with Justice sitting up and watching her owner's movements to and fro. The cats head moved as if she were attending a tennis match. It went on so long that Justice finally let out a screech causing Shelly to jump.

"What's wrong with you?"

Justice jumped off the sofa and walked down the hall and into the bathroom. When Shelly got to the door, the cat was sitting in the tub. *Meow*, she said.

Leaning against the door jamb, Shelly let out a chuckle. "Okay, I get the message. Juliet told me to relax, take a bath, drink some warm milk. I see you were paying attention to her suggestions." She gave the cat a scratch and then called her out of the tub so she could turn on the water.

Wearing a big, fluffy robe, Shelly poured some milk into a saucepan to warm it on the stove. "I haven't had a bath for years. I always shower. I have to admit," Shelly told the cat, "it was very relaxing."

When the milk was warmed, she poured it into a glass for herself and ladled some onto a small plate for Justice. "Juliet told me to stop thinking and let my mind rest so that's what I'll try to do."

The young woman and her cat headed for the bedroom where Shelly dimmed the lamp on the side table, fluffed her pillow, snuggled under her soft blanket, closed her eyes, and focused on her breathing. If thoughts about the crime or the suspects popped into her head, she gently pushed them away and thought of the resort's peaceful, blue lake and pictured herself in the middle of it relaxing on a float with her hand dipped into the cool water.

In less than thirty minutes, Shelly was sound asleep and began to dream.

SHELLY STRUGGLED THROUGH THE WOODS, panting and covered in sweat. When she emerged from the forest, a wide field stretched out before her. Trees were down, a building had collapsed, the ground was muddy ... there were grapes in the mud. Shelly tried to move her legs forward, but they felt like they were made of cement and each step took a mighty effort.

Lauren stepped out from the rubble and again, stretched out her arms to her sister, both of her hands missing.

Shelly opened her mouth, but the words wouldn't come so she said them over and over in her head. *I'm coming. Don't leave. Wait for me. Wait for me, Lauren.*

When she'd made it to within feet of her sister, tears spilled down Shelly's cheeks. She looked into Lauren's eyes and wanted so badly to hold her, but she knew she couldn't. What can I do? How can I help? What are you trying to tell me?

Lauren looked up at the sky and Shelly followed her gaze to see a dark SUV suspended in the air, twirling slowly around and around. The vehicle started to fall, faster and faster and just as it was about to hit the earth, Shelly closed her eyes.

There was no crash, only silence.

When she opened her eyes, Shelly was standing next to Lauren at the top of a hill looking down at the muddy field. A digger was parked at the side of the open space.

A scream filled the air.

The SUV was in the air plummeting towards the earth. When it hit the ground, the car made no sound, it only slipped into the large hole that waited for it. The soil closed over the SUV and the vehicle was gone.

Shelly turned to her sister with questioning eyes.

Lauren's lips curved into a tender smile and when she lifted her arm, her hand was there, and she placed it gently over her heart.

SHELLY WOKE with a start and sat bolt upright in bed, blinking into the darkness. Justice raised her head from her paws and trilled.

The field held a clue ... and Shelly was pretty sure she knew where it was.

23

As soon as she woke up, Shelly made a call to Henry at the diner and left a message telling him she'd be in to work a couple of hours later than usual. She showered, dressed, grabbed a granola bar and paused at the door to pat Justice.

"I wish you could come with, little one. Wish us luck."

Justice released a loud, clear trill and jumped onto the window sill to watch Shelly peddle her bike down the street.

After her dream, Shelly had texted Jack about going to the farm with her before work and when she woke, she was happy see his reply about meeting her there at 6am.

She arrived earlier than planned and as she

locked her bike by the food barn, Shelly got a call from Jack. He couldn't make it because of an unexpected work commitment and suggested they go the next morning instead.

With a sigh, Shelly started for the barn's kitchen to work on some pies, but stopped and turned and looked up to the hills surrounding the farm. Something tugged at her. Feeling her pepper spray in the back pocket of her jeans, she did an about face away from the barn.

Mist rose from the green fields of Glad Hill Farm under the sun's early morning light as Shelly hiked up the trails to the first bluff where she and Dwayne had stood while he pointed out the vast property of the farm he owned. Standing on the hill, Shelly looked over the expanse of greenery, fields, the apple trees of the orchard, and back to the tourist section of the farm. Looking to her left, she knew what she needed to see was beyond the fields of the orchard so she returned to the trail and headed in that direction.

The trail became difficult to navigate with vines and brush grown over the path. Shelly pushed at the low-hanging branches and underbrush. Prickers scratched at her legs as she passed. The day was warming up and perspiration dripped along her back and wet her hairline. The more she thought about last night's dream, the more anxious she became. Winded and with her heart banging in her chest, she emerged from the trail into a wide open field.

This was the spot where Dwayne wanted to start his winery until Paul shot down the idea in order to create a Christmas tree farm. Moving her eyes across the space, Shelly saw the uprooted trees, boulders dug from the ground pushed to the side of the field, the muddy tracks of the earth-moving machines that were being used to overturn the soil and add more loam to the land. Looking to the right, Shelly saw what once was a small cabin now knocked to the ground ... logs, broken windows, and boards tossed down like garbage.

That was the spot Lauren came from in the dreams.

With her arms hanging by her sides, Shelly stared, knowing full well her sister would not appear, but letting a moment of hope wash over her.

Taking in a long, deep breath, Shelly ran her hand over her face and turned away from the rubble of the log cabin to look over the land and at all the work that had been done so far to create an appropriate landscape for planting the evergreens.

Machinery was parked on the opposite side of where Shelly stood, closer to what appeared to be a dirt road leading into the property.

Looking up at the sky, she closed her eyes and recalled the details of the previous night's dream. When she imagined the car twirling overhead, a shot of adrenaline pulsed through her. Picturing the SUV beginning to plummet, Shelly's eyes snapped open and a moment of dizziness struck her so hard she almost toppled backwards.

Regaining her balance, a terrible sensation of panic pummeled her so she whirled and ran towards the woods to pick up the trail, her brain screaming at her to get out of there. Just as she stepped into the cover of the trees and brush, the engine of one of the excavator machines started up with a roar. Men had arrived at the site to work.

Shelly's chest heaved up and down and she stood for a few moments to catch her breath, thankful she'd left the field when she did. Turning to head back to the main part of the farm, Shelly halted, something pulling at her. Slowly she glanced back over her shoulder, terror nearly strangling her. Two excavators lurched over the field.

Abby. Dwayne. He must have killed her and buried her in that field.

Feeling paralyzed, Shelly forced her feet to move and she hurried along the trails back to the farm, all the while experiencing the sensation that someone was back there following her.

When she burst out of the woods to see the lake and the paths running around it, her heart began to find its usual rhythm and she slowed her pace. The petting zoo and the food barn, the building that housed the office, and the lane past the office that led to Dwayne's house .... the familiar sights caused her to breathe a sigh of relief, yet she took one last look behind her to be sure no one was lurking in the shadows.

Standing next to her bike about to unlock it so she could ride to the police station, she reached for her phone to send a text to Juliet and Jay when a voice called out to her and she turned to see the woman who worked as the office manager hurrying towards her carrying a folder.

"Shelly. You're early today." The woman, looking upset, mistakenly thought the young woman had just arrived to work in the farm's kitchen. "My babysitter just called. My three-year-old fell and hit his head and she's taking him to the hospital. I'm meeting them there. I have to run. Would you bring this folder to

Dwayne's house for me? Have you been in there?"

Shelly shook her head.

"Well, the door's always open. Don't bother to knock, just go right in. When you step inside, there's an office on the right. Just put this on the desk. Paul's working down at the Christmas tree plot. He'll be back in a couple of hours. If this binder isn't there when Paul gets in, he'll have a hissy fit." The woman extended her arm so Shelly would take the leather folder. "Could you run this down there for me, please?"

Shelly took the folder reluctantly. "Sure, I'll do it. Hope your little boy is okay."

"Could you do it now before you go in to bake? I don't want Paul chewing me out over it. He'll be angry anyway because I have to leave." The woman turned and rushed to her car.

Shelly watched her go and looking down at the leather binder in her hand, she sighed and headed to Dwayne's house walking along the quarter-mile pathway that wound past the petting zoo and a section of the planted fields of pumpkins, corn, and tomatoes. The air felt heavy from the heat and humidity and it pressed on Shelly making her sluggish.

She wanted to talk to Jay about her dream and the thoughts that were swirling around in her head making her feel ill. Was she right about Dwayne being the killer? Was she jumping to the right conclusion? Dwayne's accelerated mental slide might be from the guilt and remorse of taking a life.

When she arrived at Dwayne's farmhouse, she walked up the three steps to the porch and stood at the door feeling uncomfortable about going in without knocking. Hesitating for a few moments, she raised her hand and rapped on the wood of the screen door and waited. All she wanted was to get rid of the folder and ride to the police station.

No one answered the knock so she opened the door and stepped into the small entryway. The living area was to the left, a long hall that probably led to the kitchen ran next to the staircase. Shelly hurried into the room used as an office and placed the folder on the desk on top of a pile of papers. Turning around to go, her breath caught in her throat and she let out a gasp of surprise.

"Hello, Shelly." Dwayne stood in the doorway looking tired and disheveled. He didn't ask why the young woman was in his office. "Could you help me? I spilled my pills in the kitchen."

Shelly swallowed hard. "Okay, sure. I can help."

Seeing how weak Dwayne was, she didn't think he was capable of attacking her so she asked the question she'd been thinking about all morning. She watched the man's face for his reaction and steeled herself for his reply, certain the man was Abby's killer. "Dwayne, do you know where Abby Jackson is?"

"Abby." Dwayne muttered the word.

"Did you hurt Abby?" Shelly asked with a gentle tone.

Dwayne made eye contact with the young woman, his facial muscles hanging loose and droopy.

"Are you alone here?"

Dwayne turned and shuffled down the hall with Shelly following after. He seemed oblivious to her question, but then he answered. "I'm alone."

The large kitchen had been nicely updated with new appliances, a wide island, and white cabinets. Next to three pill bottles, a plastic weekly pill container of ten little compartments, two for each day, stood upended on the counter, pills spilled over the top and down onto the floor.

"I made a mess." Dwayne stood helplessly staring down at the floor.

"Did you take some of these pills?" Shelly

wondered if Dwayne had become confused and took more of the pills than he should have.

"I think so. I'm supposed to take a lot of them." Dwayne's brow furrowed as he struggled to kneel on the floor. He scooped up a handful of pills and brought them to his mouth.

"No." Shelly batted the pills out of the man's hand, then found a clean cereal bowl in the cabinet and knelt to gather the spilled medicine tablets and capsules. "Does Paul fill your pill container for you?"

"I guess so." Dwayne told her listlessly, and with great effort, he dragged himself up off the floor.

"Do you take your pills on your own or does Paul tell you when to take them?" Shelly asked.

"I don't recall," Dwayne said watching her.

After she'd picked up all the pills, she stood and lifted one of the bottles to read the prescription. The number of pills to take each day was scratched out and above, written in pen, was the number '6'.

Shelly looked at each of the other two containers and saw the same thing ... the pharmacy printed number was rubbed out and a new number was written above in ink.

"Dwayne, did you take pills this morning?" Worried the man had overdosed, Shelly reached for her phone in the pocket of her jeans, but before she could retrieve it to call for help, Dwayne reached for the kitchen island to steady himself.

Shelly watched the man sway back and forth. His eyes rolled back in his head before he lost his grip on the counter and began to fall. Shelly lunged and grabbed the older man's arm helping to break the momentum.

Dwayne lay unconscious at her feet.

Kneeling, she searched Dwayne's neck for a pulse. A faint beating thrummed against her fingertips. Shelly didn't realize that when she knelt and bent over Dwayne, her pepper spray had slipped out of her pocket.

"Dwayne," Shelly spoke softly. He did not respond. Panicked, she reached to her back pocket for her phone and sat back on her butt about to punch in 911.

Footsteps coming from behind her caused Shelly to look up just as Paul Blake reached down and swiped the phone from her hands. She peered up at the man as the phone skittered across the wood floor of the kitchen.

And that's when her brain cleared and all of the pieces of information snapped neatly together.

Too late.

24

Juliet woke early to prepare breakfast. She put the cinnamon buns in the oven and then, standing at her kitchen counter, she sliced cantaloupe and apples, cut strawberries, oranges, and watermelon into pieces and added all of it to the bowl to mix together the fruit salad. The waffles she'd made were wrapped in foil to keep them warm.

Checking the time, she glanced at the back door to see if Shelly was about to come in. They'd made arrangements to have breakfast together before each headed off to their jobs. Her friend and neighbor was already ten minutes late.

A sense of dread came over Juliet and she strode out of the house and over to Shelly's where she knocked on the back door. When there was no answer, she hurried to the front of the house and pounded on the door. She could hear Justice howling crazily inside.

Juliet raced back home, got the key Shelly had given her, and ran back to her friend's house. Flinging open the door, she shouted Shelly's name as she hurried from room to room with the cat at her heels.

"Where is she, Justice?" Juliet bolted to the back of the house to see if Shelly's bike was there. "Where did she go?" Running back to her own cottage, she grabbed her phone and sighed. A text had come in from Shelly before Juliet had crawled out of bed telling her to hold off breakfast until tomorrow. She and Jack were going to check something out at the farm.

"That's a relief." Juliet sent her friend a text to report that she'd already made the breakfast because she foolishly didn't look at her phone until just now. *We'll eat it tomorrow*, she texted and went to put everything in the refrigerator.

Removing the cinnamon buns from the oven and getting a container to put them in once they'd cooled, Juliet paused as the feeling of dread returned. She looked down at Justice who had followed her home. The cat hissed.

"Exactly." Juliet picked up her phone and called Shelly's boyfriend, Jack.

~

WHEN PAUL GLANCED down at Dwayne unconscious on the floor, Shelly backed around to the other side of the kitchen island slowly moving her hand to her back pocket. Her heart sank when she touched her jeans and couldn't feel her pepper spray.

Paul lifted his eyes and glared at her.

Shelly's breath was so tight in her throat that she could barely get the words out to lie to Paul. "I think Dwayne killed Abby."

"Well, you're a clever one, aren't you?" A gruesome smile formed over Paul's mouth like a big, red slash. "Dwayne *is* the killer. He confessed late last night. He was distraught." He gestured to the old man prone on the floor. "I think he tried to overdose."

Shelly didn't believe a word of what Paul said, but she tried playing along. "I think he's become despondent over the murder. That explains his sudden mental decline." Shelly took a step towards her phone. "We need to call 911."

"No," Paul shouted. "Why do you think I knocked the phone out of your hand?"

Shelly froze and shook her head.

"We're not going to call for an ambulance." Paul gave Dwayne a little kick in his side. "Let the monster die. We'll call once he takes his last breath. I'll tell the cops Dwayne confessed to the murder just before he died here on the floor. And you'll corroborate my story."

Shelly's eyes were wide and she began to shake. "You can't. You can't let him die. We need to call for help." When she moved again towards her phone, Paul sprang at her and grabbed her arms with such force that Shelly cried out.

"You aren't calling for help for this old fool." Paul sneered and his dark eyes flashed. "You won't lie to the police for me, will you? Maybe you need to follow in Dwayne's footsteps." Holding one of her arms, he dragged Shelly across the room and reached for the dish with the pills she'd gathered up from the floor. "What a shame it will be when you're both discovered dead... two overdoses in one day."

Understanding what Paul's plan was, Shelly twisted and pulled trying to break the man's grip on her, but Paul held tight and tried to yank her closer to get his hands around her throat. Shelly lifted a leg and attempted to hit Paul in the knee. Side-stepping the kick, he pressed his thick fingers against her throat and choked the air from her lungs.

WHEN JACK ANSWERED, Juliet sighed with relief. "I texted Shelly, but she didn't answer. I wanted to make sure the two of you were okay."

There were a few moments of silence on the other end of the call. "We postponed going to the farm," Jack said. "My boss called an unexpected early meeting at the resort."

Panic trickled over Juliet's skin. "Well, why doesn't Shelly answer my text then?"

Jack said, "I called Shelly as soon as I saw the message this morning. She was already at the farm. She told me she'd bake the pies since she was there anyway. That way she wouldn't have to go back in the afternoon. Maybe there's noise in the kitchen. Maybe she doesn't hear her phone."

"Maybe that's it." Juliet ended the call and stood staring across her kitchen looking at nothing.

Justice let out a growl.

Juliet called Shelly's phone and listened to it ring and ring and ring. She clicked off, grabbed her keys, told the cat to stay put, and running to her car, she pressed the screen on her phone to place one more call.

≈

DESPITE SHELLY'S wild scratching and clawing at Paul's face, the man didn't release his grip on her throat and he'd bent her backwards close to the counter. Desperate, she swept her hand over the top of the counter, her fingers finding the cereal bowl full of pills.

Shelly snatched up the bowl and smashed it against Paul's temple. He let out a gasp of air and his grip loosened on the young woman's throat. She took her opportunity and kneed Paul in the groin with a powerful thrust of her leg and the man crumpled from the two sudden blows.

With no time to grab her phone from the floor, Shelly took off running from the kitchen knowing that Paul would be after her in seconds. Making a quick decision, when she reached the front door she smashed her hand into it to make it fly open, then ducked into the office off the entryway just as the screen door slapped shut. Hoping the sound of the door opening and closing made Paul think she'd rushed out of the house, Shelly leaned against the wall of the office trying to catch her breath.

Listening for the man's footsteps, she scanned the room for a weapon and her eyes locked on to two things she needed.

Cursing, Paul bolted down the hall with blood trickling down the side of his head, pushed open the door, and ran down from the porch into the yard, his head whipping from side to side searching for Shelly.

Tiptoeing out of the office, Shelly dashed back to the kitchen, picked up her phone from the floor, and punched in the emergency number just as Paul burst into the room from the back door. The voice on the phone asked what her emergency was and she shouted, "Glad Hill Farm. Dwayne's house. Ambulance."

Leaning slightly forward, his eyes wild and crazed, Paul muttered, "I'll kill you."

Shelly planted her feet, flung the phone down, took something from her other hand, and bent her knees ready to fight. *Not unless I kill you first*, she thought.

Paul lunged.

Shelly raised her arm and smashed him across the nose with the paperweight from the desk. Blood spurted from the man's nostrils, he hesitated, but came at her again.

This time Shelly slashed at Paul with the letter opener she took from the office and before he could grab the object from her hand, she plunged it into his shoulder.

Paul screamed ... and then the cavalry kicked the back door open.

Jay, in her police uniform, along with two officers, advanced with their guns drawn shouting at Paul to freeze.

Shelly sank to her knees, trembling, as the officers took Paul into custody. Jay knelt in front of the young woman.

With her hair tangled, her neck bruising from Paul's strangle hold on her, and sweat dripping down her face, Shelly handed her two unconventional weapons to Jay. "I guess I don't need these anymore." Her voice came out hoarse and raspy, and then tears gathered in her eyes and one glistening drop dribbled down her cheek.

Jay wrapped her arms around Shelly and held her.

25

EMTs had burst into the kitchen a few minutes after Paul was handcuffed and the police officer who was administering to Dwayne moved aside for them. Shelly was taken to the hospital for examination, was treated for superficial injuries and released into the waiting arms and caring heart of Jack Graham.

WITH EARLY MORNING sunlight and fresh air streaming in through the window, Shelly and Jay sat in the kitchen at Juliet's antique farmer's table while the young woman carried over platters with pancakes, cinnamon buns, fruit salad, and a vegetable quiche. Juliet placed a saucer with a chopped up egg on the floor for Justice.

"Finally, we get to enjoy the breakfast I planned for the other day." Juliet raised an eyebrow at her friend and gave her a mock scolding look.

Paul Blake was taken into custody and would be charged with the murder of Abby Jackson. Paul attacked the young woman when she arrived home from her date with her boyfriend. He had been stalking Abby since he'd returned to Paxton Park to work at the farm. Paul had fallen for her when she worked at Glad Hill and when he approached her for a date and was soundly refused, he became obsessed with the eighteen-year-old.

The night she disappeared, Paul waited in the shadows for Abby to come home, approached her car when she was about to get out, and then jumped in and forced her to drive away.

After killing her, he buried Abby in her SUV in the acreage of the Christmas tree farm he was developing and his plan was to make his uncle look unstable, eventually uncover the hidden vehicle, and tell the police he'd found it while working on the new farm project, thereby pinning the murder on Dwayne.

Paul had been tampering with Dwayne's medication and causing him to take too many pills. He even lied to the pharmacist and said that his uncle had flushed his prescriptions down the toilet and needed all new refills, thereby getting the extra medication needed to over-medicate the older man. He also dropped clues to the farm staff about Dwayne's mental decline and made up stories about mistakes and mismanagement he attributed to his uncle for additional evidence that the man was losing it. Paul hoped that by pinning the murder on Dwayne, not only would Paul be free of suspicion, but he would then be able to take over the farm.

Jay shook her head. "We had eyes on Paul Blake, but there wasn't enough evidence to take him in," she looked at Shelly, "until you figured it out."

"I didn't figure it out until it was almost too late," Shelly said. "I was pretty sure Dwayne killed Abby."

"Adam Wall snuck out of his house that night to go meet a girl." Jay shook her head. "Adam didn't want Abby to break up with him, but he was seeing someone else on the side." She let out a sigh of disgust. "In good news, Dwayne is already doing so much better. He's still in the hospital, but he'll be released soon now that the drugs have left his system and there are no lingering effects. He was close to death when you found him. Good thing

Juliet called me with concerns about your whereabouts ... or who knows how things would have ended."

"Between Justice's fussing and my worry, I knew I had to report my suspicions that something was wrong." Juliet poured juice for her two guests. "Anyway, everything has been set right. Shelly is safe, Dwayne will be back to normal soon, and the murderer is in custody."

There was one thing that would never be right again ... Abby was gone and there was no way to fix it. That reality plagued the three women, but none of them voiced the heart-breaking truth.

"What about Paul's mother, Nora?" Juliet asked. "Was she in on the mess in any way?"

"It doesn't seem so," Jay reported. "Who knows if Paul had plans to get rid of Nora so he would become the sole owner of the farm. I'm sure he won't be sharing that information with law enforcement."

After enjoying the breakfast food, Jay put down her fork. Making eye contact with Shelly, she said, "I need to thank you for figuring out what was going on and where Abby had been buried."

Shelly tried to brush off her contribution to the crime's solution. "It was a coincidence, really."

Jay lifted her hand. "You may call it what you

will, however, my take on your help is that it is a purely natural phenomenon."

With narrowed eyes, Juliet lifted her glass about to sip. "You mean a paranormal phenomenon?"

"I don't care what name people give it," Jay said. "Shelly has a heightened ability to pick up on people's subtle clues ... their nervousness, false information, worry, fear. All the intangibles that most of us miss. It's only out of the ordinary because the rest of us don't pay attention to our intuition or to the non-verbal communication that people give off."

"What about her dreams though? And Lauren's appearance in those dreams?" Juliet asked.

Shelly sat listening to the conversation with her hands clasped tightly together in her lap. Sensing the young woman's discomfort, Justice padded over to Shelly and jumped onto her lap, purring.

Jay said, "I think the dreams are Shelly's brain working on a problem when she's at rest, putting all the little details together and making connections between them. Lauren shows up in those dreams because Shelly's mind uses her sister as a signal to alert her that the information in the dream is important."

Running her hand over the cat's soft fur, Shelly

let out a sigh. "That makes sense. I don't have any strange skills. I'm just sensitive to other people's feelings."

Adding more fruit to her plate, Juliet kidded, "Too bad. I hoped you could tell my future ... or at least, give me the correct numbers to the next lottery drawing."

"Sorry," Shelly told her friend with a grin. "I'm unable to help you with that."

"Well, I guess I'll keep you around anyway." Juliet chuckled.

When breakfast was over, the three women headed outside to walk Jay to her car.

Jay's face clouded. "Early tomorrow morning, the team will be unearthing Abby's SUV and recovering her remains. The location has been confirmed via ground penetrating radar."

Shelly's breath hitched in her throat.

"I'm glad she will be returned to her family and they'll be able to give her a loving burial," Juliet said.

The women hugged, Jay drove away towards the police station, and Shelly brought Justice inside and then rode her bike to work.

~

THE SUN ROSE JUST over the horizon when the forensics team, Jay, a few other officers, the coroner, and several others assembled on the property of the Christmas tree farm. The heavy equipment began its task with its engine roaring.

Shelly stood under some trees at the edge of the bluff looking down at the activity, wishing the machines could be quieter and more solemn as they moved the earth to find the buried vehicle and its passenger.

The terrible crushing sadness she felt made it hard for her to breathe and her heart pounded hard against her chest.

She hadn't wanted to come to the place, but she felt she had to be there to pay respects to the young woman who had lost her life.

Feeling overcome and with legs shaking, Shelly was so weak she was about to slip to the ground when she heard a rustling sound behind her that made her whirl around.

Juliet walked off the trail into the high grass and headed towards her friend. "I knew you'd be here." She stood next to Shelly and took her hand. "I didn't want you to be alone."

Gratitude filled Shelly's chest and caused tears to

well in her eyes. She squeezed the words, *thank you*, from her constricted throat.

As they were about to turn to face the field below, more sounds could be heard on the path behind them and the young women looked around to see Jack approaching from the opposite direction Juliet had arrived from.

He smiled when he saw them at the bluff, walked over, and hugged them both. "I thought you'd be here. I wanted to be with you. I didn't want you to be alone." He held Shelly's other hand and the three stood together, side-by-side and shoulder-to-shoulder, as Abby Jackson was brought back into the light.

THANK YOU FOR READING!

BOOKS BY J.A. WHITING

To hear about new books and book sales, please sign up for my mailing list at:

www.jawhitingbooks.com

Your email will never be sold, shared, or spammed.

If you enjoyed the book, please consider leaving a review. A few words are all that's needed. It would be very much appreciated.

BOOK SERIES BY J. A. WHITING

PAXTON PARK COZY MYSTERIES

CLAIRE ROLLINS COZY MYSTERIES

LIN COFFIN COZY MYSTERIES

SWEET COVE COZY MYSTERIES

OLIVIA MILLER MYSTERIES (not cozy)

ABOUT THE AUTHOR

J.A. Whiting lives with her family in New England. Whiting loves reading and writing mystery stories.

Visit me at:
www.jawhitingbooks.com/
www.facebook.com/jawhitingauthor